THE UNWORTHY

A NOVEL

AGUSTINA BAZTERRICA

translated by SARAH MOSES

SCRIBNER

New York   Amsterdam/Antwerp   London   Toronto   Sydney   New Delhi

Scribner
An Imprint of Simon & Schuster, LLC
1230 Avenue of the Americas
New York, NY 10020

First Scribner trade paperback edition March 2025

SCRIBNER and design are trademarks of Simon & Schuster, LLC

For information about special discounts for bulk purchases,
please contact Simon & Schuster Special Sales at 1-866-506-1949
or business@simonandschuster.com.

The Simon & Schuster Speakers Bureau can bring authors to
your live event. For more information or to book an event,
contact the Simon & Schuster Speakers Bureau at 1-866-248-3049
or visit our website at www.simonspeakers.com.

Interior design by Kyle Kabel

Manufactured in the United States of America

1   3   5   7   9   10   8   6   4   2

Library of Congress Cataloging-in-Publication Data has been applied for.

ISBN 978-1-6680-6370-5
ISBN 978-1-6680-5188-7 (pbk)
ISBN 978-1-6680-5189-4 (ebook)

In this town there were no mirrors / or windows /
we looked at each other in the walls /
dirtied by disasters with no origin /
the roots tangled in whips.

—Gabriela Clara Pignataro

. . . hearing the dark land talking the voiceless speech.

—William Faulkner

Can the shape of light be forgotten?

—Ximena Santaolalla

THE UNWORTHY

Someone is screaming in the dark. I hope it's Lourdes. I put cockroaches in her pillow and sewed up the slip, so they struggle to get out, so they crawl under her head or over her face (and into her ears, I hope, nesting there, the nymphs damaging her brain). I left small gaps between the stitches so the cockroaches would escape slowly, so it would take effort, like when I trap them (imprison them) in my hands. Some of them bite. They have flexible skeletons; they can flatten themselves and fit through tiny spaces, live without heads for days, survive underwater for a long time. They're fascinating. I like to experiment with them. Cut off their antennae. Their legs. Stick needles in them. I squash them with a glass so I can linger over their primitive, brutal frames.

I boil them.

I burn them.

I kill them.

*   *   *

I write with a small, sharp quill I keep close, in the hem of my white nightgown, with the ink I store under the wooden floorboards. On the pages I hide next to my skin, held by the strip of fabric I use for this purpose. There are times I need them on me, close to my heart, under my gray tunic, which was worn by the men who used to live here. We believe they were priests, monks, men of religion. Austere men who chose to live as though they were in the Middle Ages. They're dead, though some of the women say they see them out of the corners of their eyes in the dark. It's rumored that when He and the Superior Sister arrived from the ravaged earth, the collapsed world, they found neither cell phones nor computers.

*   *   *

Three of the Chosen entered the Chapel of Ascension. They were Minor Saints being brought to the altar, their hands resting on the shoulders of the servants guiding them. They were beautiful, as only those brushed by God can be. The air was imbued with a sweet and fresh scent. The smell of mysticism.

The sun lit up the stained glass and the Chapel of Ascension filled with small, translucent gems, forming an ephemeral mosaic.

A cloud covered the sky and the transparent colors dissolved. But we still saw, with absolute clarity, a thread of blood running down one of the Minor Saint's cheeks, staining her white tunic. We all knew who had done such a poor job of sewing her eyes shut before the ceremony. Mariel. Useless, helpless Mariel, wiping the palms of her hands on her gray tunic, her eyes shining as she gave us an afflicted look. I wonder what Mariel's name used to be.

The Superior Sister stood in the dark on one side of the altar. We saw her strike the light wood floor silently with one of her boots. War boots, like her pants, black, military, a soldier's. We couldn't tell if the whip hung next to her other foot. It was too dark to see it. We knew He was also at the altar, behind the chancel screen, the frame of three wood panels that prevents us from seeing Him. (Only the Chosen and Enlightened have this privilege.) He spoke. He told us that to be Enlightened we would have to relinquish our origin, the erroneous God, the false son, the negative mother, the trivial ideas, the nocturnal filth that drags itself slowly and invisibly through our blood.

I looked at the veins in my wrists and brought my finger to one of the blue lines.

To purify.

He called us unworthy, like He always does, like He does whenever we gather in the Chapel of Ascension, after three days, or nine. (We never know exactly when we'll be summoned.) He uttered the word "unworthy" again, and it reverberated against the walls, as though His voice had the power to mobilize the inert stone.

The Minor Saints sang the Primary Hymn, the original hymn and one of the most important, the one that confirms the brush of divinity. We don't understand it; the hymns are sung in a language known only by the Chosen. He explained the hymn to us again, said it speaks to how our God protects us from contamination through the Enlightened, and proclaims that "without faith, there is no refuge."

After a dramatic silence, the Minor Saints resumed their song. I saw thousands of white petals leave their mouths, filling the air, lily petals that glimmered until they disappeared. Their voices can reach the universal notes, vibrate with the light of the stars. (That's why their eyes are sewn shut, so they're not distracted by the mundane, so they capture the reverberations of our God.) Sacred crystals hang from their necks as a symbol and assurance of their holiness. Quartzes of purity, transparent gems. The Minor Saints' tunics are bright white, stainless. We listened to their voices in silence, ecstatic and relieved, the a cappella music distancing us from the chirping of the crickets, a sound like rage that lulls you to sleep.

4

The three Minor Saints resumed the Primary Hymn until they began to bleed in unison. Mariel stifled a scream and pulled out a tuft of hair. We all looked at her, our eyes lingering on her head, which was nearly bald. When she'd arrived, her hair had been thick and she had been free of contamination. That's why she wasn't relegated to being a servant. We didn't understand why she insisted on disfiguring herself. Some of us smiled with pleasure because we knew Mariel would receive an exemplary punishment. Others hid their faces in their hands, feigning prayer to mask their delight.

The Minor Saints resumed their song at the altar, but we were distracted by thoughts of who among us would be chosen to clean the blood off the floor, who would have to spend the night treating and sewing the Minor Saints' eyes, and who would punish Mariel. I'd had an exemplary punishment in mind for some time. I brought my hands together and pleaded that I'd be chosen to implement it.

One of the Minor Saints fainted, and the servants dragged her by the arms to the Chosen's quarters. The Superior Sister stood up in the middle of the altar and motioned to us. It was time to go. He remained behind the chancel screen, or so we assumed, because we never see Him leave. We don't know what He's like. Some say He's so beautiful it's painful to look at Him; others that His eyes are like downward spirals, disturbed. But these are all just guesses, because we unworthy have never seen Him.

We rose in silence, holding in our anger, hiding our rage, because it's not every day we get to hear the Minor Saints sing. They're fragile, some can't tolerate the weight of the holy words they chant (words that ensure the bond with our God is not broken). They can't endure the sight of the sacred glimmer in the dark.

I was chosen to clean the floor and not to decide on Mariel's exemplary punishment. It's rumored she'll have to strip naked, that Lourdes is going to stick a needle somewhere in her body. A good lesson. Simple and elegant. I wish I'd thought of it, but Lourdes comes up with the best punishments. They always pick hers.

Cleaning the Chosen's blood was the offering and sacrifice demanded of me by the Superior Sister.

The Chapel of Ascension was gloomy, though I had lit a few candles so I could see the red stains on the floor. The flames moved and the light they projected cast shapes on the stones, drawings that danced in the dark.

The Minor Saints' blood (like that of all the Chosen) is purer, that's why the servants can't clean it. I touched it slowly, trying to sense the lightness, the joy of being part of our Sacred Sisterhood, and the improper, subterranean thoughts being removed, those thoughts that remain of the fading earth we come from. I brought my bloodstained finger to my tongue and tasted winged insects and nocturnal howls. I understood that one of the Minor Saints was going to die. I was glad, because the most beautiful funerals are held when the Chosen pass. This time I'd have to get them to pick me.

While I was cleaning, a Full Aura seemed to float in, and she sat down on a pew. She didn't see me kneeling on the floor. I knew she couldn't hear me, but I kept still. I was ecstatic because I'd never seen one. I recognized her by the marks on her hands and feet, the transparent quartz hanging on her chest (the Chosen's quartz), and her white, translucent tunic. Her long hair covered her useless ears, their perforated drums. Noise cannot be allowed to distract them. I've heard that few exist. She moved her hands, touching something in the air.

Full Auras can discern the divine signals, the hidden signs He sends us in the Chapel of Ascension. That's why they have those marks. Understanding God's messages leaves traces on their bodies (wounds on their fragile skin, sores that never heal) so they don't forget his presence. She seemed to radiate a light capable of invoking the angels. I squinted, and in the gloom I could make out the aura that crowned her. It was perfectly radiant, lances of fire surrounded her head, vibrating of their own free will. I closed my eyes, dazzled, and felt she must live in an immaculate time when pain did not exist.

She began to orate. Her voice had the resonance of crystal shattering. I couldn't understand the disquieting, fractured language. The Superior Sister entered the Chapel of Ascension quickly, her steps like strikes, and took the Full Aura by the arm. The Chosen (the mutilated) live behind the Chapel of Ascension in quarters we can't access. Only He and the Superior Sister can, and the servants who attend them. Someone had left the door open and the Full Aura had escaped, but the Superior Sister was gentle because a Full Aura can't be disturbed while she's orating. The thread that connects them to our reality can snap, leaving them trapped in the intangible dimension, a place beyond the air. It's only happened twice. Those Full Auras were never seen again.

Some servant is going to be punished for leaving the door open. The Superior Sister will ensure she's made to scream.

She looked at me furiously, but I lowered my head as is expected in her presence, before her magnitude. I didn't want to meet her eyes. They hide an ice storm.

I finished cleaning and left for my cell, but first I walked through the hallways and took a detour to see the carved black door. No one was around, so I went over to touch the

wood. Beyond it is the Refuge of the Enlightened. They
don't live with the Chosen because they're the Sacred
Sisterhood's most valued treasure ~~(that's why they're not~~
~~mutilated like the three orders of the Chosen—the Minor~~
~~Saints, the Diaphanous Spirits, and the Full Auras)~~. The
door is in the center of a long hallway and it's far from the
cells where we unworthy sleep. The hallway is lit by candles
the servants replace every night. There are empty cells on
either side of the door that only the Enlightened can open.

I knew I didn't have much time, that it was risky, but I
ran my fingers over the wings of the angel carrying its pyx,
the lily petals, the nightingale feathers. As I imagined the
day I'd be consecrated as Enlightened ~~(and not as Chosen,~~
~~I don't want to be Chosen)~~, the day I'd be given the sacred
crystal and the door would open for me, I heard a cry that
was like a wail, and then a smothered scream, a scream like
a growl, a growl like the silent lament of an animal lying in
wait. I moved away from the door and ran.

*　　　*　　　*

I can't tell anybody I saw a Full Aura. If I do, the unworthy
will accuse me of things I haven't done, because they didn't
witness the miracle, because I dared to speak of the marvel.
The Superior Sister will send me to the Tower of Silence,

near the Cloister of Purification. The Tower of Silence (that place we fear) was built of stone along part of the wall (we believe the monks used it as an observation post), with small, paneless windows, in a circle that rises high, so high you have to crane your neck to see where it ends, the eighty-eight steps of cold stone forming a spiral staircase.

I know they would abandon me there, at the top of the Tower of Silence, with no food or water, alone, under the open sky, the crickets chirping, the sound hypnotic, ethereal, frightening. Far from the House of the Sacred Sisterhood.

In the company of bones that shine in the dark.

*   *   *

I write in my windowless cell, by the light of candles that burn too fast. With a knife I stole from the kitchen, little by little, I chip at a small crack in the wall for air and light.

I hide these pages in the bedsheets or under the wooden floorboards. When I want to save the ink left by the monks, I prick myself with needles and use blood. That's why some of the blotches are darker, a mineral red. Sometimes, I make ink out of charcoal or from the plants and flowers I gather, though it's dangerous to do so. Just like it's dangerous to be writing this, at this time, in this place, but I do it anyway, to remember who I was before I came to the House of the Sacred Sisterhood. What did I do, where did I come from, how did I survive? I don't know. Something has broken in my memory and I can't recall much of my past.

I burned many pages, the forbidden pages that spoke of her, of she who is buried with the insurgents, the dis-obedient women: Helena.

*   *   *

The haze is from the ravaged lands, the destroyed world. It's a cold haze with a sticky consistency, like a spiderweb that comes apart between our fingers. Some have had skin reactions, burning, severe pain. The skin of one of the ser-vants changed color. We haven't seen her since.

It's hard for us to breathe.

The unworthy have been making more sacrifices for days now. The Chosen have interpreted God's signs, as they always do, and the Enlightened have announced that "without faith, there is no refuge." The Enlightened antic-ipate catastrophe. They're the only ones who know God's name. The rest of us can't pronounce it, because the secret language must be learned, and it hides from us like a white snake devouring itself. To speak it is to be torn apart; it's like music composed of splinters, a mouthful of scorpions.

The haze makes it hard for us to move, but we carry out our sacrifices to reduce its damage. Some torment themselves by fasting; others walk on their knees. Lourdes offered to afflict herself by sitting on shards of glass.

The sun seems eclipsed. Its light doesn't shine; its rays give no illumination or warmth. It's as though we were living in perpetual night.

Without faith, there is no refuge.

*   *   *

The Enlightened said we had to keep making sacrifices, otherwise the air would become petrified and we'd die like fossils in the haze. We trust their messages because they possess all three of the Chosen's virtues. They're emissaries of the light; that's why they have the Minor Saints' ethereal voices, the Full Auras' prophetic vision, and the Diaphanous Spirits' perfect pitch. They're mediators between us and the ancestral divinity, the hidden God who has always existed, who predates the gods created by men.

The Superior Sister shouts in the hallways: "Without faith, there is no refuge." We cough. Spit white saliva. Tremble from the cold. The temperature has dropped even further. We're worried about the crops, which feed the Chosen and Enlightened.

I write beneath a blanket, close to the subtle warmth of a candle flame. I write with my blood, which is still hot, is flowing. My fingers hurt from the cold. Our sacrifices are important. Our abnegation helps protect the House of the Sacred Sisterhood. We're young women, with no marks of contamination; we haven't aged prematurely like the servants and have no blotches on our bodies; we have all our hair and teeth, no lumps on our arms, no black sores on our skin. Some of the unworthy have offered the martyrdom of cleaning the servants' pustules. They can't hide their looks of disgust, their contempt. They carry out their sacrifices in silence.

*　　*　　*

We've been breathing the haze for three days.

Some have begun to question the efficacy of the sacrifices. The Superior Sister has made them scream.

We moved to the dining hall at night. Its low roof and small windows maintain the heat better. The servants started a fire in the middle of the room, on the red tiles, so we wouldn't freeze. We pushed the tables that usually face each other off to the side and have been sleeping on the mattresses from our cells.

We let the servants sleep with us so they don't die of cold. We need them to serve us. I don't know how the

Chosen and Enlightened are sleeping, but they're our most valued asset, that's why I have no doubt they're being looked after.

I had to sleep next to Mariel, who was smiling because the haze had delayed Lourdes's punishment of her. She whispered what María de las Soledades had told her, which is what Lourdes had told her, which is that the tongues and teeth of the Enlightened are yanked out, as uttering God's name requires a void. She also confided that others say they hear screams coming from behind the carved black door, from the Refuge of the Enlightened. I think I've heard them too. Sharp cries, muffled shrieks. Mariel also told me, contradicting herself, that their practice involves biting screws or chewing shards of glass. I don't think any of it's true. Or it could be, nobody really knows about them (once one of us becomes Enlightened, we don't see her again). All we know is that there are few of them and that being Enlightened is the highest aspiration and the greatest responsibility. Thanks to them, the venom that flows through subterranean rivers, the poison that resides in the tissue of plants, the toxins carried by the wind from one place to another, don't infect our small world.

They're behind the carved black door, protected, and only He can touch them.

The haze is increasingly dense. The Superior Sister has summoned us to atone with our blood. Flagellations, cuts, lashings so our God protects us, so the haze doesn't kill us, so the natural disasters cease to plague the House of the Sacred Sisterhood.

*   *   *

After eight days the haze lifts, disintegrates. The temperature rises. We go back to sleeping in our cells. In the middle of the dining hall, there's a black stain from the fires. The servants haven't been able to remove it.

It's rumored we lost some of the crops, that some of the crickets died, though not all of them.

My back is scarred from the lashings Lourdes gave me, because the Superior Sister was busy with the other unworthy.

I know Lourdes enjoyed every minute of it.

She tried to hide it, but I saw the sparkle in her eyes. She also struck Mariel with a whip the Superior Sister gave her. And as she did, she said this wasn't Mariel's punishment, that she'd get her punishment soon. Very soon.

My sacrifices weren't enough. Lourdes had to whip me.

Without faith, there is no refuge.

✳   ✳   ✳

Now that the haze is no longer a threat, I can check the animal traps we set among the trees, in the place that begins where the garden ends. Maybe it's pretentious to think of it as a ~~woods~~, but that's what it's called at the House of the Sacred Sisterhood.

Sometimes, to preserve the few animals we have (which I've never seen), the Enlightened and Chosen eat a bit of flesh from a hare, which a servant tastes first to ensure it's not contaminated. There are very few hares, and most are deformed. A hare might be missing an ear, as though nature didn't have the drive to make it whole. Or it's a leg that's missing. Or an eye.

The traps were empty. The Superior Sister breeds crickets that provide us with the necessary protein, though we tire of eating their tiny, crunchy bodies, even if they are clean, free of venom, thanks to the Enlightened. Without faith, there is no refuge. While they eat apples, carrots, cabbage, fresh food, we eat cricket soup, cricket bread, cricket snacks, crickets with turmeric, spicy crickets, crickets prepared with all the herbs the monks kept years ago. I no longer feel their legs on my tongue, or their antennae. But I do feel them chirp in my mouth. A sound that rasps, a dangerous sound.

I thought I saw a human silhouette, shadows among the trees. Something or someone hiding. A wanderer maybe, a woman who was able to dig under the wall. But I didn't stick around to find out. I can't risk contamination.

I no longer remember when it happened. A wanderer climbed the wall without falling, but then she couldn't get down. We brought over a ladder and watched her careful descent. When she touched the ground, we stepped back and the Superior Sister told the wanderer to follow her. She would have to go to the Cloister of Purification. We could see she was starving, weak. She looked at us, uncomprehending, an expression on her face that could have been fear or repulsion. It was clear she spoke another language, though she didn't say anything. On the surface, she seemed intact, she had all her hair, no marks. We passed the cemetery with the old gravestones, the ones with the monks' names on them. She tripped, could hardly walk. No one wanted to help her up.

We reached the Cloister of Purification, a small house surrounded by trees, built close to the wall and isolated. It's where we all go before we're accepted, and it's not a cloister, though that's what we call it. It's where we hear the crickets for the first time without knowing what they are and think it's our minds losing control, that it's the sound of madness. It's where the shadows of the monks lurk, their voices in the night, in the dark. Some die, sick with contamination and sin (with loneliness). The wanderer was isolated there, and the servants fed her, as is required of them, since no one cares if they become infected, and none of the unworthy are willing to make that sacrifice. If the servants refuse to look after a wanderer, the Superior Sister goes for her whip.

The wanderer died. She died trembling, her eyes blind, covered with a white patina. Her tongue was black. The bodies of the corrupt are burned at the edge of the small ~~woods~~ space next to the wall. We believe the servant who cared for her was also burned, burned alive, because the Superior Sister wouldn't risk contagion. No one remembers who she was; they're not given names. The wanderer could have been Chosen or Enlightened because she didn't have any visible marks of contamination. I'm glad she didn't survive.

The House of the Sacred Sisterhood does not permit the entry of men, children, or the elderly. He tells us they died in the many wars, or of starvation or sadness. But I know the few who made it to the wall were killed. We all know it. The Superior Sister saw to it personally. The Superior Sister sees to it personally. We're forbidden from ringing the bell when the wanderer is a man. Immediately we let her know, and she orders us to our windowless cells. Whenever the wanderer is a man, we hear shots fired. We never see old women or children to rescue.

One of those buried in the wild cemetery of the heretics, of the cunning, one of those who no longer has a name, or a gravestone, only trees and earth to cover her aberration, one of those women let a man in. She didn't tell the Superior Sister or any of us. She hid him under the altar's wooden planks. Gave him part of her ration of food and water. She kept him there, so well hidden, for weeks; we never learned how many. But one day we noticed she was radiating the treacherous aura of disgrace, the malicious aura of betrayal. She thought she could conceal it under her tunic, but we noticed her womb swell with sin, with vice. When she tried to flee, the bells were rung, and all of us, the servants and unworthy, went after her. There was no escaping. We found her in the Tower of Silence. She'd climbed the stairs, opened the hatch to the upper floor, and that's where we saw her. We saw her walking desperately under the open sky, among the bones of the Chosen (the bones that shine in the dark), and we saw her leaning against the crenels and looking down, gauging the distance between herself and the ground, deciding whether to jump into the void or beg for her life. But we trapped her.

Diligently and patiently, the Superior Sister made her scream, made her wail until she confessed. She's said to have pulled out some of the woman's nails or some of her teeth. Or all of her nails and all of her teeth. The story goes that she broke various whips. That she yelled at the servants to bring more branches. "More, more, more," she howled. "Blood atonement." Her fury was transformed into a whisper: "More, more, more." She struck the woman so many times that some believe she killed her. We never found out what happened to the man who lived below the altar. Today, the woman is covered with earth, absorbing the dark in the cemetery of the ~~wretched~~ negligent. We all agree she should have thrown herself from the Tower of Silence.

Long ago, I too was a wanderer. I only recall this time in nightmares, and I don't remember what came before it. I only know that I was almost dead when I got here—Helena told me so. I dragged myself to the main gate and couldn't knock on it. She was the one who let me in, Helena, worshipper of the erroneous God, the false son, the negative mother, she who is now rotting belowground like the other unworthy, her mouth open. She who was compassionate enough. She said she'd seen me from the bell tower, from afar, crawling. Helena the dreamer, the reckless one. She rang the bell and told the Superior Sister, who decided not to open the door, to leave me there, because she assumed I was dying, a waste of time. But ~~fearless~~ undisciplined

Helena waited until she was alone, opened the gate, took me by the wrists, and dragged me in without help. She rested my head against the wall and gave me water, just a little. She was sensitive like that, cautious. Had she given me a lot of water it would have done me harm.

When I was able to get up, we walked to the Cloister of Purification, near the Tower of Silence and the cricket farm. She stayed with me, feeding me and risking contagion. The Superior Sister punished her disobedience with a month of degrading jobs, but she didn't kill her, because she saw in me a candidate for Chosen or Enlightened. Helena cleaned latrines, treated some of the servants' wounds, cut wood, massaged the Superior Sister's feet. She had to make her sigh. I know she took on those sacrifices joyfully; I know she never held them against me.

I wonder if the silhouette I saw ~~in the woods~~ among the trees was real or if I imagined it.

*   *   *

He told us that to be Enlightened we had to cease being inhabitants of the dust, emissaries of filth, an incessant hive of misunderstanding, an outpouring of transgression. He warned us that He could sense the lugubrious sickness lurking in our bodies. María de las Soledades laughed.

We all knew it was because of the word lugubrious, which was like lucubration, salubrious, lubricious. He stopped talking. The Superior Sister got down from the altar with alarming speed and put a spiked cilice around María de las Soledades's mouth. She took her time, was thorough and diligent. The muscles in her arms bulged and I saw the satisfaction in her eyes, and her horrific beauty, which always disorients and captivates me, like a tempest. When she tied the cilice behind María de las Soledades's neck, the belt's spikes broke the flesh of her lips.

No one looked at her again, but we knew blood was running from her jaw to her tunic and that she'd closed her eyes to hold back her tears, to stop herself from crying out in pain. We knew she would have to wear the spiked cilice, the stigma of disgrace, for a week or longer, and that none of us would offer to disinfect her, or give her any liquid, because we all knew (we whispered) that María de las Soledades stank of chemicals, fermented fat, rotting vegetables. We believed she didn't deserve to be among us, that there was something sick about her, something contaminated. The Superior Sister will no doubt force one of the servants or the weak to look after her, but we won't care. While her martyrdom lasts, we're going to judge her silently.

It was raining. The drops slid down the stained glass in the Chapel of Ascension. I imagined that each contained a small, twinkling universe, absorbing the colors of the glass. The different shades of green in the luscious garden, the sky blue, the yellow and violet flowers, the white of the deer that seemed to have tears in its eyes. I looked at the deer's majestic antlers, like the branches of a tree, and at the tip of each horn, where there is a circular symbol we don't understand. The drops sparkled like suspended cells. I touched the blue vein that bulged on my wrist and wished for my blood to retain the light of the world.

To purify.

The stained glass was smeared with black paint. The glass with images of the erroneous God, the false son, the negative mother, the God unable to contain the avarice and stupidity of his flock, the God who let them poison the nucleus of the only thing that mattered. This God, who left us adrift in a poisoned world, cannot be named or looked at.

Mariel entered the Chapel of Ascension slowly, her head lowered and her tunic stained. She had two aureoles at the level of her chest. We knew they were blood, because Lourdes had stuck the needle in her nipples. When they told me, I clutched my fists so tightly I slit my palms. I would never have thought of that. Mariel held a black paper rose, which meant that someone had died. Some shed two-faced tears, tears of happiness, because a funeral means days of preparation and delicious pastries.

The Superior Sister saw Mariel, got to her feet, and then we lost sight of her for minutes that seemed endless. When we heard the bells toll, announcing a death, we stood in silence. It had to be one of the Minor Saints. I wanted it to be. I prayed. I begged with all my still-impure heart, my unworthy heart.

On the way back to my cell, I passed María de las Soledades's door, which was open. I saw Élida lying on the floor and María de las Soledades stepping on her head. Élida was pleading with little yelps because she doesn't yet know the language spoken at the House of the Sacred Sisterhood, our language. Some have to learn it when they arrive. Élida was learning it and she shouted things like "Leave me, please, beg of you, offering, yes? I care of you." It was funny to hear her speak, on the rare occasion she did. María de las Soledades seemed to be smiling, though she couldn't move her mouth. There was pleasure in her expression as she applied a little more pressure to Élida's head with her shoe. Élida was crying. María de las Soledades had found her weakling and wanted to see her suffer. She looked at me and I held her gaze, judging her in silence, until she lowered her eyes.

When I'm in my cell, I can't help but look at the empty bed with no sheets on it. Helena isn't here anymore, but I don't miss her. You can't miss someone who oozed indecency, debauchery. She was a worshipper of the erroneous

God. Wayward. Nor do I long for her beauty, which was like a claw stroking you slowly. Sometimes I lie down on her bed and fall asleep thinking about what would have happened if she hadn't found my writing. She read all the profane sentences, all the forbidden words about her voice, her impure magnetism. I had to get rid of the evidence.

Every morning I rise and seek her scent, a scent like a song, like a wildfire you long to burn in. But I can't smell it anymore.

Now no one says her name. It's hard for me to remember where she's buried, with no tombstone or flowers. The barren grave of a wayward woman. I can't hear the screams, the pleas that disappeared under the earth that fell on top of her. I don't know if that night I went to the cemetery of the cunning, the obstinate, the heretics, where the graves are lost among the trees. To the land of the untamed. I don't know if it was all a dream.

I was barefoot and hid in nooks and crannies to avoid the Superior Sister. The cold, hard slabs dug into the soles of my feet, and then I felt the softness of the wet grass, the drops in my hair. I don't know how I crossed the garden, I don't know how I didn't trip over the buckets we use to collect rainwater, I don't know how I made it to the field and beyond, to the far reaches of the wall, where the grass gives way to brush and the trees become something like a ~~woods~~

wild garden. I don't know if I dreamed under the rain, lost, counting the trees in the dark, trying to remember where I was, looking for the tree with the hollow in it, our tree. Our haven hidden in the thicket. That's where she was, buried next to that tree, our tree, touching its roots. I don't know if I dug, pleading for forgiveness, crying. When I found her, her mouth was open and full of dirt. I lay down by her side and screamed. I thought I could smell her scent mixed with that of the wet earth. I don't remember if I put the chain with the gold cross around her neck before I kissed her eyes, before I removed the dirt from her mouth and closed it, before I covered her. We'd found that cross in her mattress; she'd so desperately wanted to hide it. I don't know if I slept in the thicket. I returned to my cell without having been discovered. I don't know how.

I hear the mourning bell toll. We have to put on our veils and go to the garden. First, I'm going to bring my hands together and beg that a Minor Saint has died. I'm going to plea

*　　*　　*

He was watching us silently from the bell tower, or so we believed. We saw a black silhouette framed by the shimmering sky. The cupola refracted lights and it looked like

26

He was surrounded by a spectral rainbow, but we couldn't be sure it was Him. The veils only allowed us to make out shapes and colors. The Superior Sister ordered us to get down on our knees. I felt the cold soil through my tunic, felt it rise up my legs. We lowered our heads, mute, patient. First we heard the radiant sound of a green and translucent sea. It was the trees, the leaves moving in the wind. Then He said: "You are she-wolves engendering poison, a battalion inseminated by perdition and atrocity, a sack of fetid putrefaction, a seedbed of disgraceful lucubrators. Unworthy, homicidal women." His voice resonated in our bodies, as though He were not up high, as though His presence permeated the garden. As though He were everywhere. "One of the Minor Saints was murdered and her sacred crystal stolen." A dense and surreal silence settled in among us, and as though our shock could halt the natural movement of the world, the leaves in the trees stopped fluttering. Lourdes's dramatic and calculated wail shook us from our trance. It was followed by moans, cries, shouts. Fainting spells. Some struck their chests, others clawed at the earth, pleading for forgiveness. They pulled out their hair and scratched at their faces, leaving deep gashes. I smiled behind my veil.

An icy breeze picked up and we shuddered. It smelled of cold (remnants of the haze), though it was a warm day. The Superior Sister stood and watched us for some time. She was attentive to the spectacle of feigned suffering. When she looked at me, I pretended to pass out. Enough, she said, almost inaudibly, but the word was like a dart that wounded us one by one. We went still and then composed ourselves, stood up, neatened our tunics, and listened to her. She took off her veil and some of the women covered their mouths with their hands. Doing so is forbidden, the punishment is walking on glass. The Superior Sister went over to Catalina and told her to take off her veil. We understood we were to do the same. She waited for each of us to uncover our faces before taking a small bell from her pocket and ringing it. We looked at each other without understanding what was happening. This bell was new.

One of the servants brought the Superior Sister a whip. It was a branch, flexible and painful. The servant hid a smile because she knew someone was going to scream. The Superior Sister chooses her whips carefully; they have to be resilient, to last as long as possible. She goes into the place she calls the ~~woods~~ to find them. The place that begins where the garden ends, the garden to the left of the House of the Sacred Sisterhood, opposite the Cloister of Purification, the Tower of Silence, and the cricket farm. The Superior Sister spends hours choosing branches to hit us with. She tests them on tree trunks, leaves behind wounds, lesions that ooze translucent blood: red, green, amber. For special punishments, she selects one of the leather whips the monks used to flagellate themselves. It's an ancient whip with nine leather thongs.

The servants brought Mariel forward. Her hands were tied and she was barefoot. I heard whispers and smothered cries, but the Superior Sister made a slight movement with her head and we were silent. Mariel's white nightgown was stained with blood. It's certain they stuck more needles in her nipples as punishment, because Mariel was in charge of looking after the Minor Saints during the ceremonies, that's why she now had to atone with her blood. The white nightgown (which was increasingly red) revealed the shape of her body, and though she was gagged, we heard her screams clearly. She screamed something in one of the languages that's forbidden in the House of the Sacred Sisterhood. All I could make out were words, the odd sentence, that I bring myself to write just as I heard them: *"Salu, Marie, plen de gras, vousette beni entre tute lay fam."* Her feet were dirty with soil. They had put a white bonnet over her head, shaved what little hair she had to humiliate her further. She was trembling. I wondered what fear smelled like. I thought you wouldn't be able to sense it, because it's like a body turning to ice on the inside.

Under her nightgown she was naked.

The Superior Sister went over to Mariel and struck her on the mouth because the forbidden prayer in the forbidden language was increasingly clear. Mariel was silent for a second, but in a very soft voice she went on imploring the negative mother, the false son, the erroneous God. In her fury the Superior Sister turned Mariel around and pulled off her nightgown, which fell to the floor. We all covered our mouths, feigning horror at the spectacle we'd seen time and again. Mariel trembled. We saw the needles stuck in her body, we saw the trickle that was red, almost black. Some discreetly placed their hands over their chests to protect them (as though that were actually possible).

The Superior Sister likes to build anticipation, so you never know when the first blow will strike your flesh, when you'll have to atone with your blood. She wants to educate us in the art of agony.

One: the sound of the whip was soft, almost imperceptible, but it left a mark of raw flesh on Mariel's back and drew the first drops of blood.

Three: open wounds, vivid red.

Six: Mariel's cries stunned us, but under them, we could hear a subtle change in the Superior Sister's breathing, the rhythm accelerating, turning into something else. A moan.

Eight.

Ten. The atonement.

Ten strokes meant red flesh, a fever, infection, possibly death. We covered our eyes with our hands. We didn't want to see her collapse, but Mariel couldn't hold herself up and fell to her knees. We thought that was it. Mariel would also have intuited this. Maybe she felt a certain relief, but the Superior Sister ordered the servants to pick her up off the ground. They tied her to a pole surrounded by branches and trunks, lit them, and she blazed.

She was incredibly beautiful. Like a firebird.

*   *   *

Mariel didn't kill, but Mariel blazed. That's the mantra the servants have begun to murmur, the nameless servants. They whisper poison because their bodies carry the marks, the signs, of contamination, and though they can no longer infect us, they have to work to clean our filth and the filth that runs through their veins. They hate us because they have to serve us. The marks are the remnants of the pustules, wounds, infections. The rashes are the filth of evil, the filth of collapse, the filth of failure. This filth absorbed from the sick earth has blighted them permanently, lest we forget that corruption lurks and the Enlightened are the only ones who can quell it. This filth, nesting in the servants' skin, in their cells, is the anger of the sea, the fury of the air, the violence of the mountains, the outrage of the trees. It's the sadness of the world.

They wear old, torn tunics. Faded tunics, the colors indistinct. They sleep in what was once the monks' library. But now there are no books. They don't have beds, just blankets they throw on the floor. I went in once, out of curiosity, but left disgusted. It smelled of rage, as though there were thorns in the air, but that's not why I left. I left because the shelves with no books took my breath away, and a sharp pain struck my chest, though I can't explain why.

The servants aren't punished enough.

*   *   *

Lourdes joined up with her favorites (the ones that follow her everywhere, her weaklings) to organize the Minor Saint's funeral. Despite the sweltering heat, I spent the whole afternoon looking for cockroaches in the kitchen, patiently, diligently, while I pretended to sweep. (I offered this sacrifice, which is the servants' task.) I'm going to grind them up and sprinkle them in Lourdes's sheets so she sleeps on their white, viscous blood.

Ever since the Superior Sister saw me with the Full Aura, she has demanded more sacrifices and offerings, things I shouldn't have to do, that only the servants do. Nobody says no to the Superior Sister. Nobody who wants to remain alive. Except fo

*   *   *

Sometimes I have to stop writing because I hear noises, because the ink runs out, because sleep overcomes me, because I hear the Superior Sister's steps. But I always find moments to keep at these words I form in secret, on these rusty, sand-colored pages streaked and stained by time. I'd hidden them in the Cloister of Purification (far away, three thousand steps from the House of the Sacred Sisterhood, but within the wall), under some floorboards. Now they're with me again, and I run my hands over them, smell them. They're mine, part of this book of the night I can't stop writing.

These words contain my pulse.

My breath.

*   *   *

There's something sick in the wind, a warm stupor of venom and insects. A curse creeping out of the devastated lands. We can feel the vibration of something destructive coming into being. It's not the haze, it's something else. A plague rising from the black zones, the ravaged, barren lands. We first sensed it in the dining hall as we broke our cricket-flour bread. Something was throbbing in the air, silent and bestial. We shuddered.

The Chosen didn't warn us about this poison. Neither did the Enlightened. The borderless wind had appeared silently, undetected. "This is a test," shouted the Superior Sister as she stood from her raised chair, where she sits to watch us eat. She stepped down, dragging the branch-whip she keeps next to the chair, and ordered us to cover the cracks in the doors. She placed a handkerchief over her nose. We all did the same with napkins. Some tried to stifle cries and coughs, their eyes filling with tears. The Superior Sister shouted: "We must overcome this test, the Enlightened are testing our faith." She struck her whip against the floor. And then, suddenly, she was quiet. The door to the dining hall opened and a shadow appeared. We couldn't see who was there, though we recognized the voice.

From the darkness, He spoke to us almost in a whisper, His voice like a subterranean river overflowing: "How do you expect the Enlightened to protect this lot of apathetic, unworthy women? Why would they bother sheltering mis-trustful, skeptical, inconsiderate bitches who drag them-selves through the earth, filthy and drooling like a pack of blasphemous, suspicious, wavering women? Without faith, there is no refuge." He lingered on the word bitches as though He was savoring it, biting into it.

He left and the servants got to work slowly, clumsily. They were dazed by the wind. Some rested their heads against the walls to settle their nausea, others fainted. No one helped them up.

I looked closely at Lourdes. Lourdes with her butterfly skin, radiant and pristine, and those hands, so light and perfect, yet sharp. Insect hands that inflict pain. Lourdes, who arrived without signs of contamination, with all her hair, with no blotches on her face. With her teeth intact. She's got to be rotten on the inside, otherwise she'd be Enlightened or one of the Chosen, a Minor Saint, a Full Aura, a Diaphanous Spirit, but she's just one of us, one of the unworthy, one of those who wait. Lourdes tried to hide her pallor, that of a wounded bird sipping slowly from its dish, as though she could cover up her desperation. The funeral might fail, and she knew it. We all did. Despite the sick air, the vomiting and the headaches, we felt an over-whelming joy at the possibility of seeing her fail.

When I reached my cell, I vomited blood, but I smiled.

*   *   *

The wind stopped suddenly, my vomiting as well. A thick calm settled in, a fragile relief. We passed the test, the women whispered. The Enlightened will go on protecting us, they said. Without faith, there is no refuge. Lourdes resumed preparations for the funeral, and the Superior

Sister sent me to hunt for mushrooms to make special pies. She said: "I want fungi from the ~~woods~~." I lowered my head and, without correcting her, said that my offering would be to look for the best fungi. What she wants is the fruit body, and what she calls the ~~woods~~ is a space within the wall, where the trees grow next to each other, blocking out the sunlight with their evergreen cloak, where the damp cold envelops you slowly like a cutting murmur, like a rumor capable of destruction, and nature expands until the stones of the wall hold it back. That's where she is. ~~The fearless~~ The undisciplined one: Helena.

On the way to ~~the woods~~ the grove, I always turn left after the House of the Sacred Sisterhood. I stop by the garden where we grow our crops, hoping to see a Diaphanous Spirit. There was one there. She was crouched down, her head on the ground, listening to the insects' almost inaudible, manifold language. The sacred crystal was off to the side of her neck. Diaphanous Spirits wear radiant, white tunics that are always spotless. I don't know how the servants manage to remove the stains of dirt. She heard my steps, or maybe my tunic brushing against my skin, or maybe the impure blood flowing through my veins. I stood, watching her, and she rose to her feet. Diaphanous Spirits can see inside us, they don't care about our appearance. They try to listen to us, it's what they do whenever they're being observed. That's why no one dares watch them. They can perceive the bitter, lurking sound of sickness, the slow absorption of bone tissue; they've heard the soft swell of the dark where our organs reside; they can tell by our pulse whether our heart seeks only possession or wants to redeem itself, whether it seeks to wound or to dissolve into another heartbeat; they can discern the damp movement of the bacteria that inhabit us, the microcosm we carry around without feeling it. Sometimes they spend long hours in the field trying to detect human words in the wind, messages from our God. It's common to see them turning in circles, the palms of their right hands open to the sky and the left to the earth. But no one knows why they do this.

She opened her mouth, and I could see the black hole, her teeth, but not her tongue. When they're Chosen, their tongues are cut out, because they're only permitted to communicate what they know in writing to the Superior Sister. ~~I don't want to be Chosen because I don't want to be mutilated.~~ They like to disgust us, to make us flee at the sight of them, but they don't bother me. I watch and try to learn because some say the Diaphanous Spirits can hear our thoughts.

Before I entered the space that longs to be a ~~woods~~, I took off my shoes and lay down in the grassy garden to feel the sun on my skin. What sound does the sun make? A hot din? A calming whisper? There were no clouds in the sky. It made you want to touch the blue, to hold it in your hands, to feel its velvety beauty on the tips of your fingers. I saw a butterfly fluttering too close. It was azure; its wings seemed to give off white light, but its beauty burned. Its fiery legs left marks when they perched on your skin. They were toxic.

I noticed something move in the grass. I sat up and watched two ants closely. They had trapped a cockroach and were now towing the body (which was thirty or ninety times their size), one ant per antenna. The cockroach's legs twitched; it intuited its fate. To be devoured by thousands of ants.

Do cockroaches feel fear?

It was hot but not sweltering. I took a breath. When I had nightmares, Helena would sometimes put her arms around me. I think I used to dream of life before (I like to believe I remembered it in dreams), life before crossing the wall, life on the sick earth, when I was hungry, and didn't have a stream with running water, or pastries, or a God. When I was a wanderer. The life I can't remember consciously, no matter how hard I try. I'd cry out in my dreams because of the confusing images, because of the things I didn't understand but that hurt me, and though I'd open my eyes, I'd enter a state of paralysis and struggle to breathe. It was as though the automatic mechanism of inhaling and exhaling had failed, as though my mind didn't know how to carry out such a simple act and had just resigned itself to waiting until I choked. But Helena would put her hands on my face, one on either side, and look me in the eye. When she was able to calm me down, she'd lie next to me and hold me until I fell back asleep. Ever since we buried her alive, ever since the earth covered her up, ever since nobody, except for me, has been able to tell her nameless grave apart from the others, I haven't dreamed of life before.

Suddenly, I thought I saw a shadow among the trees, some way off. I asked myself if it could have been a wanderer hidden in ~~the woods~~ the thicket, or a spirit, one of the monks that hound us.

*　　　*　　　*

I know the difference between edible mushrooms and poisonous ones, that's why I'm sent to hunt for them. I know I learned to recognize them, but I don't remember how. Sometimes I save the red ones with white spots, the amanitas. A few days before the Minor Saint's death was announced, I gave Mariel a tiny piece as a test, mixed it in with her dinner. She spent the night licking the wall in the hallway that leads to our cells. The Superior Sister struck her, shook her, but Mariel didn't react. She looked at her with empty eyes. Some whispered there were wicked spirits in the air and that Mariel was susceptible to letting them in because she was mentally weak. The spirit of the monks, someone said, almost inaudibly. The Superior Sister tired of striking her and left. Some of us tried to get Mariel to react. Everyone seemed afraid she would die, or worse, that she would infect us with the dark spirits, because it was already clear to all of us (except me) that something sinister was taking shape in her eyes. Catalina screamed and said she had smelled Mariel's poisonous breath, that when she'd shaken her, something immoral had tried to lodge itself in her womb. The unworthy moved back, horrified. I looked at Mariel, fascinated by the amanita's effect. I wondered what would happen if I gave someone a lot more. How unhinged would they become? The unworthy grew bored, left Mariel alone, and she went on licking the wall until her tongue began to bleed. I took her away and led her to her cell. Not out of mercy, but out of curiosity. I wanted to see the extent of the amanita's effects. I helped her change, laid her down in bed, and waited for her to fall asleep. First she tried to tell me something, but her tongue was swollen. I understood the odd word: "Enlightened, there are, ~~woods~~, none." She was delirious.

Mariel didn't kill.

Mariel blazed.

While I hunted for mushrooms, I checked the traps we hide in strategic places and kept walking until I heard the joyous and sparkling sound of the water in the Creek of Madness. He says God provided us with this secluded haven, this small, pristine Eden with clean water that surges from the center of the earth, or from the celestial and invisible hands of our creator. We don't know, don't understand, logically, how the miracle occurs, we just accept it. Without faith, there is no refuge.

In the Creek of Madness, we found fish with empty sockets instead of eyes. We cooked them and fed them to a servant who had blotches on her body, hardly any teeth, tufts instead of hair, a voice like a parasite. She didn't want to eat them, but we forced her. An abomination for the abominable. That's what Lourdes sang as we opened the servant's mouth and put pieces of fish in it, black fish holes. She didn't die, but she told us that her chest had gone up in flames. Her blood was lava, a scalding ocean, disintegrating her. Her veins were threads of fire. We heard her screams for most of the night, until she grew quiet, and we thought she'd died. Afterward she told us it was as though she'd been in the Creek of Madness all night, submerged in the water (which in her delirium was black), watching bolts of lightning glide like eels, her hands and feet bound by algae, unable to move, drowning, surrounded by headless eyes that floated and stared at her without blinking. No one wants to eat those fish.

I felt a damp chill. I kept walking but couldn't find any amanitas, which I wanted for Lourdes, to see her lose control, make a fool of herself. Strip in the dining hall or the Chapel of Ascension. Run through the garden. Bite the Superior Sister, or pull out her own soft red hair. Lourdes dancing unbridled, wild. I found chanterelles, but no trumpets of the dead. They would have been so fitting and glorious for the funeral pastries.

I saw ivy berries, which are poisonous but good for making ink, so these words are a different color. Bloodred, charcoal black, indigo, ochre.

I write as though I were there now, as though I could experience it again. I try to grasp each of the seconds that made up that time, believing I can thread them together with these fragile symbols. The feelings return so clearly when I write that I don't doubt the faithfulness of my memories, my fabrications. I try to capture that present, that now, but it blurs with every word drawn, every time I use this insufficient language. Because I'm in this present, which will always become the past, barren words on a stained page. Now I'm in the kitchen, barefoot, in the gloom, alone. Now I'm writing at the table, by the soft light of the embers, alert to the sounds of the night, always alert, because these pages must not be found.

Yesterday they went through our cells. I'd known a few days earlier and was prepared, because I'd recognized the vibrational flow, the whispers and half smiles that start to appear when the servants know they'll have the luxury of humiliating us. But my cell is immaculate, and they bore easily. One servant stood there looking at the crack where I've been chipping at the wall, but thought nothing of it.

Today, when I finish writing, I'm going to hide these pages and the knife behind a cabinet in the kitchen, wrapped in the fabric I use to protect them, the fabric I tie around my waist, under my tunic, where I keep the pages and my knife (which I use to open the crack) when I'm on the move, when I sense someone could find them. Tomorrow, when I organize them, number them, I'll put them back in my cell. Maybe one day, in some future now, someone will read what I have written and learn of our existence. That we were part of a Sacred Sisterhood and lived on a sliver of land that remained pure, resplendent, thanks to the piety of the Enlightened. Or maybe they'll become dust and return to the earth, fertilizing it, nourishing the roots of a tree, and our story will be understood through the leaves that oxygenate the collapsed world.

Now I breathe the cold air in the desolate kitchen, an icy cold like the tip of a needle. Now a cockroach twitches its legs and antennae, trapped in a jar. It's dark red and I think it's beautiful because of the perfect repugnance it rouses in me. It's a small work of living art. How long will it survive without oxygen?

To seize the ephemeral, savor it.

I look at the veins in my left wrist.

To purify.

Now I return to another present, to my sharp memory. I write in that present to relive it, to be there again, as though the moment were trapped in a circle of eternity. I move slowly. I enter a different climate, the air thick, and I feel like I'm breathing inside the crazed heart of the ~~woods~~ thicket, like I can sense the wild vibration of a place unable to expand. That cannot expand. I see some milk caps. I crouch down to gather them and notice an unusual movement nearby. A dead bird is decomposing. There are so few that I decide to pay it homage, to observe death at work. The grass around the corpse is dry, the bird's fluids having drained down to nourish the earth. The creature looks framed by an aura that could protect it from further death, as though nature has given it a prominent spot because of its sacrifice. A personal sanctuary. The cells have been destroyed and the volatile substances have traveled through the air. The ritual has begun. Flies and beetles feed on it and deposit their larvae in its hollows, in its open mouth, in its wounds. They eat its flesh, its tissues, its eyes, its organs, in a minute, frenetic dance. Together, silently, they shred the bird. They produce a smell that's rank and heavy. I can also smell the perfume of dead flowers. (I wonder if God is inside the larva. Our God, whose name we don't know. ~~I wonder if God is the hunger behind hunger, and if behind God lurks the hunger for another God.~~) I wonder what stage of death she's in, under the earth, if she feels her body disappearing little by little in the darkness that covers her. If she's defenseless. The bird died looking up at the sky between the leaves in the trees. Or looking up at the stars. It died surrounded by beauty. Helena died in the dark, she died in the disaster. She was the one who taught me that disaster means living without stars, or celestial bodies, or comets, without the light of night, in complete darkness. ~~(In the mouth of God?)~~ She wrote it on the palms of my hands with her finger covered in mud. We were in our secret tree, inside the hollow, sitting on dry leaves, our arms around each other because we barely fit. In our secluded, hidden haven. Near where they bury the insubordinate. First she wrote *des* on my left palm, then *astrum* on the right. She brought her lips close to mine and said in a whisper: *des-astrum, no astro*—no stars. Almost all the bird's feathers are gone because other birds have taken them to their nests, as they did with some of the larvae to feed their chicks. When there's no more flesh, the flies, beetles, and ants will clean the bones, diligently and patiently, and they will do a thorough job of eating the weak larvae, those that can't be converted into anything else.

In the distance, I hear the wasps. The sound announces harm. Wasps bite with tiny jaws and sharp teeth. They have a retractable stinger, which means they can sting as many times as they want without dying. There's a nest on a tree branch. I've seen it before, high up, but I don't interfere. One day I found a dead wasp, intact, and I kept it. It was so pretty, elegant like a monstrous flower.

I keep hunting for mushrooms until I see her. She has fainted, is struggling to breathe, and there are wounds on her dirt-smeared hands. Around her head are a few amanitas. The red of the mushrooms contrasts with her black hair strewed in the grass. I sit down to observe her carefully, from a prudent distance. She doesn't have any signs of contamination. Her skin is immaculate, resplendent. She's wearing a light dress that could have once been white but is stained and frayed. Filth has drawn strange figures on it, an ominous design. The fabric is heavy and covers her knees. Her legs are riddled with small scratches from thorny plants. She has on men's boots, they look like combat boots, no doubt too big. She probably stole them from a dead body. You can tell she fled something, someone, it's the same with all of us. I don't see a bag or backpack. The unworthy arrive as lost causes. The servants too. We were all wanderers before we came here. It's likely she found a gap in the wall and dug at it until she reached the other side. She won't have been the first. Some knock on the gate with the last of their strength until we let them in. Others think they can climb the wall, but they break their necks when they inevitably fall. The shrewd ones look for the weak points, the gaps.

I continue to observe her. She's majestic, like the white deer in the stained glass. Could she have been the silhouette hiding among the trees? Small circles of sunlight filter through the leaves and move slowly over her dress and skin. A dragonfly perches on her stomach. I cover my mouth so I don't cry out with joy. I haven't seen one in years. I'd thought they were extinct. Through the transparent architecture of the dragonfly's wings, through that fragile cathedral, I see the wanderer's breath grow steady, though it's still slow. She radiates an otherworldly light. I move just a little closer, and the dragonfly takes off. The wanderer remains unconscious. She smells of sweat and dirt, but strongest is the scent of something sweet and fierce, like the blue of a limpid sky, a blue like a precious stone. Something that can envelop you, enchant you, split you open with pleasure. A paradise at the edge of an abyss. I have to leave her. She looks like the perfect candidate for Chosen or Enlightened. But I worry she's on the verge of death, because I sense in her breathing the vibration of agony. Maybe she's full of sin, infected on the inside. I approach her slowly to cut off a piece of amanita. She opens her eyes.

At first she doesn't see me. She's dizzy or confused and her vision seems blurred. I stop in my tracks, hold my breath. When she realizes I'm too close, almost touching her, she drags herself away, looks at me, opens her mouth, her eyes, and screams silently. I put two amanitas in my tunic pocket and stand up. I run without giving her a chance to follow me.

*   *   *

Today is the Minor Saint's funeral. There are whispers that the Full Auras spat and frothed at the mouth, that they trembled for hours, were racked with spasms, possessed by words indecipherable to the rest of us. It's said the Diaphanous Spirits translated the subterranean messages of fire ants. They can detect the glimmer, the red gleam that the ants' tiny bodies give off. This means they saw signs, that's why the Superior Sister sent me to hunt for mushrooms. He communicated the news early. He told us of shimmering birds and exotic flowers that had sprung up overnight. He announced that there had been flashes in the sky, that the gates had opened to receive the Minor Saint. He ordered the funeral to be held that afternoon. Lourdes said the signs indicated it should take place at sunset, the symbol of twilight and thus of death. The audacity of Lourdes. She announced the ~~corny words~~ good news solemnly.

Lourdes managed the final preparations efficiently. We detest her. The temperature dropped suddenly, and as we inhaled the gray, frigid air, we collected flowers, insects, feathers, leaves. We didn't find any exotic flowers, though we looked for them. She requested fruit from the trees in the garden. There wasn't much, and most of it was bitter. The best fruit and vegetables are picked for them, for the emissaries of the light, and the rest is given to the animals (we don't know where they are). The goat milk is also for the Enlightened. And the eggs, which are so precious; once cracked open, the yolks and whites are often black or bloodred. So the servants say. The few healthy eggs are a treasure for the Enlightened alone (though I haven't seen the eggs the servants speak of).

The Superior Sister gave Lourdes permission to go into the pantry, which is where the preserves and herbs have long been kept, since the monks lived here, the worshippers of the erroneous God, the false son, the negative mother, those men that some hear at night. She rations the preserves and herbs strictly. We made pastries with the mushrooms and prepared a banquet with what little we had. We ground coffee beans. They were almost black, iridescent, tiny cells of pleasure. Some of the unworthy didn't recognize the heady, biting smell because they'd never had coffee.

When everything was ready, we groomed ourselves. Though it was cold, we felt delight, joy almost, as we bathed, because the servants brought us rainwater, not the water from the Creek of Madness. It's a special day, that's why the water has to be pure, cleaner, free of residue. Through wet nightgowns I could see thin bodies, ribs protruding like mine. Years of famine leave marks, signs, traces of anguish. A few days ago I washed my nightgown in the creek. I did it to remove the ink stains from the hem, where I hide the quill I use to write these words.

The word Rain stood out on María de las Soledades's back. I wondered if it still hurt. I know, because I was there, that when they changed her name to María de las Soledades, she wouldn't accept it. She tried to protest, said she wished to be called Mercedes or Victoria or Rain. That's the word she used: wish. We looked at her, disconcerted.

We held back our laughter, covered our mouths. Rain? The Superior Sister went up to her silently. As she walked, the oxygen around her disappeared. She devoured it with every step. It was difficult to breathe because her perfect body, her magnificent and terrifying presence, took in all the air. With a swift, almost undetectable movement, she pulled off María de las Soledades's tunic, tore it in half, and forced her to kneel down naked. María de las Soledades started to cry silently. The tears fell onto the tiled floor. She tried to cover up her indecency, but she couldn't. The Superior Sister asked to be brought one of her whips and a knife. First she struck María de las Soledades, and then, diligently and patiently, she wrote Rain on her back with the knife (leaving a permanent scar), and walked away without saying a word. María de las Soledades didn't move.

We left her lying on the floor, unconscious from the pain. But first, each of the unworthy spat on her back. Insurgent! Lourdes shouted at her. In the hallways, Catalina asked in a low voice why they'd chosen the name María, the name of the negative mother of the false son of the erroneous God. Now it's a new name, Lourdes told her, like yours, like mine. New, pure, emptied of what came before. But later, Lourdes made sure the Superior Sister found out about Catalina's question. The Superior Sister went for her whip.

As we groomed ourselves, someone whispered a song like honey flowing, like lights dancing in the sky. Singing is forbidden and punished with two days in the Tower of Silence, but no one called the Superior Sister to report the infraction. Only the Minor Saints sing, and only the sacred hymns. Lourdes wasn't around to denounce us, to ruin the moment of fleeting harmony, of precarious happiness. We all felt relief. As though it were a true sisterhood, we washed each other's hair, combed it, smiled at one another. We were silent as we savored the crystalline scent of flowers. We put on the clean, white tunics the servants had left us, the ones we wear on special occasions.

Each of us returned to our cell to reflect on the death. That was the Superior Sister's order. Now we're waiting to hear the bells that will announce the start of the funeral.

I'm not thinking about her, about her long legs, about the possibility of her being alive, finding the path back to us. I'm not thinking about the wandering woman, about the white deer with the stained dress and men's boots. I'm not speculating about the stains, about their different shades, about what caused them. I don't know if that filth is blood, mud, the splattering of violence, of intimidation, traces of hunger, desperation, loneliness, the vestiges of evil. I don't imagine myself resting my head on her stomach to hear her breath, nor do I believe I can smell her scent of a free bird, of a precipice. I don't wish for the funeral to be interrupted. I don't wa

*   *   *

The Minor Saint was lying on the altar. Sunset is the best time of day in the Chapel of Ascension because it fills with radiant specks. They're intangible, fleeting, but we're drawn to that beauty, to being in the midst of the translucent colors, to feeling saved in the splendor.

We sat down and lowered our heads to wait for the Superior Sister's signal. I had to repress a look of disgust; the Minor Saint's body was clearly rotting. Some brought their hands together, feigning prayer, to cover their noses.

We imagined Him behind the chancel screen, perceived His presence. But He was silent. He didn't say anything for so long that the silence materialized, took on density. A sharp density that shattered the air, cracked it open. We kept very still and breathed slowly, taking great care not to be wounded by the transparent shards. The message was clear, the assassin was among us women and He knew it. But they weren't going to do anything else, neither Him nor the Superior Sister. They had done it all to Mariel.

Mariel didn't kill, but Mariel blazed.

The silence began to suffocate us, and the sharp edges of broken air multiplied dangerously. Someone tried to stifle a scream, but it was so loud that we all raised our heads and saw her. A Full Aura was at the altar. One of the Chosen. The Superior Sister remained seated, monitoring what she had planned in advance. The Full Aura radiated an explosion of light, motionless flames, a red melody that blinded us for a few seconds. She was still and seemed to be looking at us, though she wasn't. Then she shook her hands with precise movements, as though she were destroying the sharp edges of the space, as though she had the power to prevent us from experiencing pain. We saw the marks on her hands. The sign of having been brushed by God. She opened her mouth and said something in a voice of brilliant, elusive immensity. No one understood: her words are not for us. She touched the Minor Saint's body and we thought we saw a blue luminescence abandon it. The Full Aura seemed to rise a few centimeters off the floor, as though she were levitating. Then her eyes rolled back and she fainted. The Superior Sister stood, unperturbed, unsurprised, lifted her up, and took her behind the altar to the Chosen's quarters. That's how strong she is, how imposing.

Some say that long ago, before the great catastrophe, the Superior Sister was a climate migrant, that she was part of an army that fought in the water wars, the wars that coincided with the disappearance of many territories, many countries, beneath the ocean. Some whisper she's not a woman, they say she could break your neck with one hand, crack your back in a single movement, that she was taught to breed edible insects in the millenary tribes, that He is her brother. I believe it all, except I know she's a woman. I know ~~because~~

When the Superior Sister returned, she stopped in the middle of the altar and motioned to us. We stood and formed a single file, then walked barefoot to the Minor Saint to pay our respects. The cold of the tiles stung like a burn. When it was my turn, I bowed my head, but not as low as I should have, because I wanted to see her. She was covered in the few flowers we had been able to gather. Most were scentless, pale in color, ailing. She was clean, beautiful almost, with feathers in her hair and a white tunic on, but decay and stench seemed to be concentrated within her, consuming her every fiber, destroying what she was. The rot had swollen her womb, though the Chosen are pure. ~~Was it the fermenting contamination that had caused it to bulge?~~ A paper beetle had been placed over each of her eyes, the emblem of resurrection. Lourdes and her artificial symbolism. In her dead hands, the Minor Saint held a stone, a sky quartz, to replace the sacred crystal that had been stolen from her. It was blue, translucent, with microscopic streaks that formed a small, encapsulated galaxy, a contained universe. I don't understand how Lourdes found a semiprecious crystal. As I returned to my seat I looked at her. She was radiant because she knew the stone would surprise us, that the detail made this the best funeral to date. I wanted to kill her, I felt this as an urgent necessity, but I sat down, and once again bowed my head. I calmed myself with the thought that I would steal the quartz that night.

He didn't participate in the rest of the funeral.

Resigned, the servants handed us lit candles, lowering their heads so we wouldn't have to see the marks on their bodies, the stigmas of contamination, so that when we looked at them, we weren't disgusted. We walked in single file to the garden. We were surprised to see the deep blue sky, implacable, the clouds in flames: orange, copper, some red, an ancient red. Others were pink, one black. The perfect sky. It was neither hot nor cold outside. There was plenitude in the air, a subtle intensity. (Was it a sign? The sky unfolding in color to announce that the gates had opened to receive the Minor Saint? Nature ignoring the very catastrophe in which it was submerged?) The cool grass was a relief when I stepped on it. I wiggled my toes and smiled, covering my mouth.

Lourdes's eight favorites (her weaklings) had the honor of transporting the Minor Saint to the Tower of Silence. They carried her on a plank, over an altar cloth embroidered with flowing shapes. The Minor Saint lay on different types of leaves, and Lourdes placed a crown with the prettiest flowers on her head. A butterfly flew over her body. Its blue wings were beautiful. We sighed with delight and admiration, until it perched on the Minor Saint and burned the corpse. Lourdes shooed it away with her hands. Many hid their pleasure at seeing her fail, at seeing that her work was now imperfect. The six burn marks from the butterfly's legs won't disappear.

We turned right and walked slowly, carefully, because we were barefoot, the clouds darkening little by little, our surroundings harder to make out with every passing second as the candles burned down. We kept the requisite distance of thirty steps from the Minor Saint. We passed the cemetery where the monks are buried, reluctant to walk through it. Some say they've seen shadows, heard screams in the night, cries like wails, hushed sounds, the howls of suffering animals. Others whisper they can sense the monks' spirits everywhere. At night, they see presences and shadows, hear voices in the hallways. We passed the Cloister of Purification (which we think was the watchman's house, though they decided to call it a cloister, despite there being no columns, no arcade, no monks moving through it).

When they reached the Tower of Silence, Lourdes's weaklings opened the iron door and climbed the circular staircase, shouldering the corpse. I was glad I wasn't one of them. There were too many steps for so much weight. Lourdes led her weaklings by candlelight. Later we learned (because she made sure to discuss the ritual again and again) that she had opened the hatch at the base of the Tower of Silence and confirmed that the Minor Saint was well-placed, balanced on the bones of the Chosen. The rest of us remained down below, waiting for the ritual to end. We heard the chirping of the crickets. We're forbidden from going to the cricket farm, but it was close. Servants keep watch day and night. Some say that beyond it lies only the wall that encloses and protects the small universe of the Sacred Sisterhood.

When we left, we didn't check whether the door was locked because it's unthinkable that anyone would go to the Tower of Silence of their own volition. The door is locked with a key when one of us has been punished, when one of us deserves to be left outdoors, under the open sky, with the hatch bolted and the bones of the Chosen and Enlightened as our only company.

The Chosen and Enlightened must preserve their purity, that's why they're not buried. Their essence is inviolable, sacred. The Minor Saint's body will be exposed to the elements because the earth's pollution must not be allowed to contaminate her. The sun, the rain, the wind, a bird or two, maybe a vulture (if they still exist) will ensure her cells, her flesh, her essence, are scattered throughout the sky, remain up high, untouched and clean. He says it's one of the greatest honors, that only the Chosen and Enlightened have this privilege.

That's why Helena, the insurgent, the agitator, the tenacious woman, is in the earth, because her body was a disaster zone, a blind maelstrom.

The banquet was a silent celebration. We had to appear sad about the Minor Saint's death, solemn and dismayed, but we were allowed to eat without restriction, to taste different flavors, and the joy in the air was palpable. I didn't want to look at Lourdes, because I imagined she was radiant in her triumph, smiling without moving her mouth, feeling that her chance at being Chosen or Enlightened was getting closer. We ate the mushroom pies the Superior Sister had made with cricket flour, which has a slightly sweet, mild taste like dried fruit, some say; like almonds, María de las Soledades said, but we gave her confused looks. How could she have eaten almonds? How can she bring herself to speak with the marks still on her face? The wounds left by the spiked cilice that haven't disappeared. The marks of disgrace. We continued to look at her, slightly disgusted. Someone said that the rain didn't speak and we laughed, covering our mouths. María de las Soledades shed a few tears, but no one heard her cry, no one cared. Catalina whispered that cyanide smells like almonds, but not everyone can detect it, said someone else, and then they went quiet because the Superior Sister rang her small bell.

I imagine an almond as a treasure that María de las Soledades doesn't deserve.

We were served the coffee. I took in the powerful aroma, the scent of danger, but also of wild joy (like what you might smell in the jungle, I imagined), and before I tasted it, I had to close my eyes. I saw my mother dancing barefoot in the kitchen. I was looking up at her from the height of my ten years. I remember her polka-dot dress, threadbare but clean, her long, shiny hair, her laughter like tiny crystals clinking in unison, her hands touching the rays of light that came in through the window. She was dancing because we were going to eat, she was singing because she'd gotten coffee and bread. That was when I still had a mother who taught me to read and write; who handled books with care, saying they were marvels contained in paper, calling them our friends; a mother who celebrated life through small acts, every day; whose luminous presence found beauty in the world that was degrading minute by minute. A world where water was scarce, and there was no school, no electricity. A world of floods, in which eight months of rain fell in less than an hour, and we lived on the roof of our house for days until the water went down, and sobbed when we saw our friends floating in the filth—Lispector, Morrison, Ocampo, Saer, Woolf, Duras, O'Connor—their pages soaked, useless, though their words were inside me, the words my mother urged me to love, even when I didn't understand them; the shifting of the earth; the tornadoes; the winds of more than a hundred kilometers an hour; the fallen trees; the animals walking in circles for weeks, for months, nobody able to explain it, until they went mad from exhaustion and died; the destroyed city; the hailstones like fruit fall-ing from the sky, exploding like bombs, projectiles of ice fracturing the fragile veil of civilization; the ruined crops; the extreme heat, fish cooked alive by the broiling sea, fish dying of thirst in the rivers, the droughts, the water wars, the shortages, the hunger, the thirst, the collapse, my mother dead in the same kitchen she'd danced in a few years prior. The sunless kitchen, its window boarded up, without coffee or food, without water or electricity, full of fear. I touched her dry hands, kissed her forehead, covered her with a dirty cloth, and left. I didn't cry.

*   *   *

It's late. I can't go to sleep because I have to look for the stone. The quartz in the hands of the dead Minor Saint, the universe it contains. The unworthy will fall asleep later than usual tonight because of the coffee, but I don't mind waiting in this windowless cell. I wait and continue to carve at the hole in the wall, continue to widen the crack to let the light in. It won't be long before I reach the other side, the night air.

The memory of my mother struck me like a blow, like a revelation, and the person I had been, the girl who couldn't cry, the teenager constantly on guard, the predatory woman who had lived in me, hidden away, came back to life. I lowered my head to stop the tears. I didn't want anyone to see my weakness, but then, then I remembered we were at the Minor Saint's funeral and I cried openly, without hiding it or feeling shame.

I cried over the school I hadn't gone to, the books I hadn't read, the siblings I didn't have, the father I'd never met, and over my mother, resplendent and rigid on the cold floor of a kitchen that no longer exists, a house that collapsed in the tornadoes, the floods, the earth incapable of supporting the cement. I cried over my small, insane family, the other family that accepted me and looked after me, my family of tarantula kids, who I left one night to look for food and found dead upon my return. The adults had killed them one by one in their sleep. Some with their eyes open, their gaze petrified in a look of fright, because they'd felt pain from the machetes and knives; they'd felt fear. When I closed their eyes, I realized their bodies were still warm. They hadn't had time to resist or scream.

I stayed with them a few seconds longer to place coins over Ulysses's eyes, the useless coins he'd given me the day the tarantula kids had taught me to pick locks, the day we'd broken into the abandoned National Library, before we'd taken the books to make bonfires, when we'd hid and I'd read them a story about a girl who'd been invited to a house where a tiger prowled from one room to the next, and the entire family had to be very careful so they didn't end up in the same room as it. I had to explain what a tiger was, and they were amazed that an animal like that had existed in the world. We took it for granted that they had died, all the tigers, that they had died of contamination, died of thirst, or by drowning, died with their tongues black and their eyes blind, died of sadness, died in the cracks of the earth, in the silent cry of the world splitting in two.

When I reached the end of the story, they danced in silence. We couldn't shout or clap, but dancing silently was how we celebrated. Almost none of them knew how to read, only two of them could, slowly and poorly for lack of practice, because they were children born into a world where all you could do was survive. They weren't lucky enough to have known my mother and her love of books.

That night, before the bonfire, Ulysses set aside the book with the story and announced that it was not to be burned, that he wanted me to keep reading, and in front of everyone he gave me some coins, the ones he'd held on to as though they were still worth something. I read another story about a man who threw up bunnies. Ulysses sat beside me, and as I read, he did impressions of the man puking bunnies. We held in our laughter until we clutched our stomachs, they hurt so much, and tears fell from our eyes, because we had to be careful not to make any noise. That was the day we called ourselves the tarantula kids.

Tobías, one of the youngest kids, said he didn't want to be a bunny, and Ulysses told him that we were tarantula kids, piranhas, scorpions, serpents. Tobías opened his eyes, without understanding. What are scorpions and piranhas? Dangerous animals, I told him. Animals that bite, sting, wound, kill. Tobías smiled. We all smiled. Ulysses put me in charge of books for the bonfires. I became the most efficient at getting my chores done, just so I'd have time to go to the library and pick stories and myths to read around the bonfire each night. I tried to pick books about politics or math to burn, or those in other languages, or translated into them. Burning a book made me angry because I knew I was setting fire to a world. But we needed to keep warm and to cook the animals we hunted. Most were abandoned pets that trusted humans too much. At first I didn't want to eat them, I couldn't, but as the days passed and I began to ache with hunger, I became the best hunter. Sometimes, when we weren't lucky, it was rats. When we ate the bits of meat we'd managed to hunt, I'd think about what the rat had eaten, and I'd have to hold back the vomit. This rat could have fed in the city's dumps, I thought, as I watched its tiny body barbecuing over the flaming books. We no longer looked through abandoned dumps for items or expired cans of food because it was too dangerous. They were watching. The adults, the plague that wanted the books in order to burn them, that wanted our reserve of water, wanted the garbage, wanted to break us.

My family was dead. I couldn't bury them, couldn't say goodbye to each of them. I had to flee because the adults were coming, they were looking for me. They knew there were twelve of us, and we knew there were far more of them. That they were armed. We knew they were cruel like us, but that they were not loyal to one another like we were. We who treated each other's wounds, who shared our food and water equally, who slept with our arms around each other to keep warm. We who were capable of dying for one of our own. We took turns spying on them and saw what they did to the children in their group. We saw the marks on their weak bodies, their empty, dead eyes. We saw the stupidity and the malice. We were quick and clever. Lynxes. But violence won. I panicked because they were close now, I could smell them, the vile stench of their filthy bodies, the rancid flesh hanging from their murderous teeth. I looked at Ulysses for the last time, stroked his forehead, drew aside the lock of blond hair covering one of his eyes. I knew the adults would take his coins, but I wanted them to know I had evaded them, that I had escaped their claws, and their victory was not complete. Ulysses looked like he was sleeping. I wanted to kiss him on the lips so his journey to the other side would be less lonely, but I heard a sound, something crunching under a human foot, and I ran.

I also remembered Circe. But I can't write about her, not now, because it hurts. It hurts too much.

(Should I be happy I survived starvation? And the years I was part of a group of predatory kids—of fierce, merciless, piranha kids? Orphan kids who couldn't trust adults. Tarantula kids who learned to hunt rats, cats, birds. Should I feel guilty about the food I stole, the people I hurt? Should I punish myself for those I killed?) I no longer care if someone finds what I've written and they read about my hardships, my atrocities. I write them down now in the indigo of poisonous berries. In the present without calendars, in the present of these pages.

I drank the coffee and cried because I was here, in this place, protected, but without my friends. With the Sacred Sisterhood. Lourdes gave me a hateful look because she wasn't able to shed the tears that would have made the funeral a resounding success, crowned it. The Superior Sister approached and put a hand on my shoulder. I couldn't bring myself to touch her, but I looked at her with the customary gratitude. Lourdes lowered her eyes and chewed her pie furiously because she was the Superior Sister's favorite. Lourdes knew what the gesture meant, we all did.

*   *   *

Circe. My enchantress.

*   *   *

When it was very late, I left my cell, barefoot so I could walk silently, hide in the recesses and merge with the dark. I walked through the hallways to the Refuge of the Enlightened. Though I knew it was a risk, I stopped in front of the black door. Slowly, I touched the chiseled nightingale's feathers. I imagined my ascension to Enlightened and closed my eyes, resting my head on the wood. I tried to hear the gouge reverberating as the wood-carver whittled the bird, likely centuries ago. I closed my eyes and focused on the sound of the wood cracking inside itself, on the expansion and contraction of the cellulose. On the mute cry of the tree the moment it was felled. On the stealthy bite of an insect. But I couldn't hear a thing. There's no one here, I thought, and it was then that someone spoke. It was Him. His voice was like the dark blue of swallows in flight, the swallows that nested in our roof during the spring, the roof of a house where I'd been happy, and that no longer existed. A sound very different from the one He makes at the altar, when He orates in a voice like a sacred battalion, a blessed legion, a voice that contains howls, that captivates and wounds in equal measure. When I heard Him close to the door I fled, but before I did, I heard a soft, broken cry.

The moon was full, bathing the garden in white, cutting light. The grass looked like a sea of glass, like crystal. I thought I saw a shadow moving among the trees. I wondered about the ghosts of the monks, who some say (whisper) were killed by Him and the Superior Sister. Some are sure the monks are not in the cemetery but buried in the garden, that the few fruits and vegetables that grow are fertilized by the holy flesh of these innocent men, that at night, hypnotic

Gregorian chants can be heard, chants that could drive you out of your mind with their beauty and voracity, chants that declare we are intruders and that the monks are waiting for the moment to return and seek their revenge. Some women swear the ghosts leave marks of fire on their bodies, finger-prints on their skin, bruises they can't explain.

I heard a scream in the dark. A bird? There are so few. Could it have been a cry? I hid behind a tree and waited. There was no one. I inhaled the fresh air and calmed down because all I heard was the chirping of crickets. Distant but constant, like water dripping, scathing, corrosive.

When I reached the Tower of Silence I saw the door was open. I remembered that Lourdes, ever cautious, solici-tous, had closed it, though she hadn't locked it. I entered and felt the hard stone of the staircase, ice-cold under the soles of my feet, and the filth that Lourdes and her entou-rage hadn't been able to clean. Something sticky and old had stained those steps. The musty smell of decay and damp was disconcerting. I don't know what I'd expected. How else would a tower built centuries ago smell? I thought I saw something move under the staircase, but I kept climb-ing (eighty-eight spiral steps). The heavy hatch took me a while to open. It hurt my hands, though I felt no pain. I'm writing gingerly now, because the quill brushes the small cuts from the splinters that pierced my skin.

When I was finally able to open the hatch, the cold night air was like an echo repeating itself. There was no respite, the entire tower seemed trapped in a bubble formed by the sound of death. By the reverberation of death's exhaustive and secret work, by the music of its silent jaws.

I made out the silhouette of the Minor Saint.

I walked on the Chosen's bones. Carefully, so I wouldn't cut my feet.

It was hard to breathe because I was inhaling the Minor Saint's particles. Her gradual disappearance from this world settled into my lungs. I smelled the deterioration and solitude. The immense solitude of the Chosen's lifeless bodies, a dim light forever on the verge of going out.

First I bent down and touched her belly. It was swollen. Hard. Then I touched the stone between her hands. They looked like claws frozen by rigor mortis, but her fingers were broken. Right, I thought, they'd had to break her bones to place the stone in her hands. I couldn't see the quartz's deep blue, but I had to have its contained vibration, its motionless galaxy. I put it in the pocket of my tunic and walked carefully down the staircase. When I reached the last step, I saw her and screamed.

*   *   *

I had to stop writing because I heard noises in the hallway. I hid these pages under the mattress, blew out the candle, and lay down in bed. Someone opened the door to my cell and stood there watching me in silence. I assumed it was the Superior Sister, the only one allowed to walk the hallways and check the cells at night. The only one allowed to open a door without announcing herself. To stand there watching us for hours while we sleep. To enter a cell and leave it the next day. ~~Like she did with me once, which I'd rather not remember, or write about~~.

She came into my cell. Her feet struck the ground even when she didn't want to be heard. Her steps are like wildfire. I couldn't see her, but she was there, filling the space with a hurricane's rage. With those war pants, those long, slender hands that look fragile but are lethal, that face, its features hypnotizing you like a goddess of chaos and destruction. Her dark silhouette violated the night, voided it. But there was something else. She stank. (Was it the crickets? Some say the dead crickets give off a repulsive smell.) She reeked of something dense, like the color black, I imagine, like excess, confinement, dementia. But I didn't hold my breath because her smell was also fiery, magnetic.

It's said (whispered) that she can see in the dark.

She stood by my bed, watching in silence until a noise distracted her in the hallway and she left.

My fingers were stained with blue ink, the ink kept by the chanting monks, the ghostly monks, which I use now and then when I can't make my own. If the Superior Sister had inspected my cell, ~~if she'd looked under my sheets,~~ I'd have had major problems, possibly an exemplary punishment, even a definitive punishment. But she didn't, and now I'm in the cleaning room, where we keep the brooms, buckets, and rags. I can write until the candle burns out. Sometimes I try to keep going in the dark, but I no longer want to waste paper or ink on incomprehensible ideograms. Someone might read me, read us. There are times I think that none of this matters. Why put myself in danger with this book of the night? But I have to because if I write it, then it was real; if I write it, maybe we won't just be part of a dream contained in a planet, inside a universe hidden in the imagination of someone ~~who lives in the mouth of God~~.

Each of these words contains my pulse.

My blood.

My breath.

If I write it down, she returns to the present of my memory. I see her clearly. She was there in the Tower of Silence, and I screamed because I didn't recognize her. I thought she was one of us, that she'd ventured into the night with the same idea I'd had. A thief like me. One of the unworthy keen on holding a small, detained galaxy in her hands. I thought she was some sort of presence, the Minor Saint's spirit claiming her mortuary stone, her payment to cross the River Acheron because she was no saint. But then she approached, and I smelled her wild and sweet scent. It was the deer. I looked at her in silence, without understanding.

I'd thought she'd died.

Died among the trees, died in the thicket. That she'd died of hunger, and of thirst, sick with sin. Died of sadness, swollen by contamination. Died like so many of the wanderers who come here from the ravaged wastelands.

I didn't know what to say, how to react. But then she spoke, and her voice wasn't radiant or translucent, wild or sweet. It was something else, the yellow gaze of a wolf, the ones I'd seen in the abandoned books at the National Library. A sad, profound voice, of someone who's experienced and accepted terror, of someone able to create beauty.

She said she'd been walking for days, parched and with no food, when she saw a wall, then a hole in the wall, and had used branches and her nails to make it bigger, that she'd hurt herself scraping at the hard earth, the stones in the hard earth, and had bled, but she'd dug for hours and had been able to crawl through, and had crossed a ~~woods~~ where she'd seen a woman in a tunic, a woman who had left her there, and she'd tried to follow this woman but had gotten lost and fainted from exhaustion, that it had taken her a long time to leave the ~~woods~~, and she'd waited until night to find a hiding place, that she couldn't bring herself to knock on the door of what looked like a convent, and she was thirsty, she repeated, and hungry, and wanted me to help her—when she regained strength she could work, do whatever I asked of her.

A gap in the Tower of Silence's stone wall let in the light of the full moon. Her skin seemed to radiate flames of ice. She got down on her knees, brought her hands together, and begged me with a forbidden sentence. I moved her hands apart violently and struck her on the cheek. Never, I shouted, ever, name the erroneous God, or his false son, or his negative mother. And this is not a convent. This is the House of the Sacred Sisterhood, where the Refuge of the Enlightened is located. They could burn you, they could bury you alive, I whispered. Then I realized I had touched her, that she could be contaminated, and in another unconscious act, I brought my hands to my open mouth to hide my desperation. I took three steps back, eight, to distance myself from her, but she approached and began to whisper sentences in another language. I begged her to stay where she was, since she could be contaminated. I would help her under one condition, I said, and only if she followed my instructions. I warned her that she could speak the House of the Sacred Sisterhood's language and no other.

I heard a chant or a scream or a wail, and looked up at the sky and saw it was close to dawn. She stood still, but then she wrapped her arms around her body as though she was freezing, or wanted to protect herself from what I was about to say.

In the darkness of the Tower of Silence, I told her I was the one who'd found her, that it would have to be our secret. I'd had the goodwill not to kill her, I said, and had left her there to see if she'd survive. Now she would have to remain in the Tower of Silence for another day, though I'd bring her food and water. Otherwise, if anyone saw her, she could be killed.

Don't leave me,

I'm afraid.

She begged me, translucent yellow, like a wolf. But I knew too well that mercy was like silent dynamite; it lodged itself in your heart until it went off, and then there was no chance of gathering the pieces. The tarantula kids had taught me that. Without mercy you survive. Without mercy there's more water for the others. Without mercy there's time to read stories about women who fill candies with cockroaches. But with Circe I showed mercy. And she did with me. The white deer is not Circe.

She saw that I wasn't going to cave, that I wasn't going to give in to her golden voice. Don't leave me, she pleaded, and told me she'd climbed the stairs, but didn't open the hatch because she'd heard voices. Men chanting, calling to her. They want to do harm, she said. There is rage in this place.

She was clearly out of her mind with hunger and exhaustion, and I told her so. How could she know about the monks? I ordered her to stay where she was, to wait, to keep silent. When I moved toward the door, she crouched down and wrapped her arms around my legs. I smelled her fierce and sweet scent. The paradise at the edge of the abyss, the crystalline blue.

She cried out words I didn't understand: "*Por fevor, telorego. Por fevor.*"

I told her to let go of me. If she wanted to stay alive, I said, she couldn't speak forbidden languages; they would yank her tongue out. She gave me a terrified look, and after seconds that seemed like encapsulated minutes, centuries contained in years, she got up slowly and went to sit down on one of the steps, crying.

I explained that she had to hide because the sun was rising, that I would bring her water.

When I left there were traces of orange clouds in the sky. In the distance, near the crops, I saw a Diaphanous Spirit. I snuck behind a tree and moved as slowly as I could so she wouldn't hear me. She placed her head on the ground to capture the sounds of the dawning earth, the delicate work of the insects, the hidden messages sent from tree to tree through their roots, and I stepped inside without her seeing me.

As soon as I reached my cell, I washed my feet with water from the Creek of Madness. The servants bring us this water every day. We drink different water, as do the crickets, the dew collected by the Superior Sister in the inverted pyramids she won't let us see. They're guarded. It's said they're glass pyramids, that the glass concentrates the dew and the water drips down a hole into a bucket, which is how she collects it. Some maintain the pyramids are made of cloth and the system is much more complicated. It used to be said (whispered) that this was all a lie, that we were just drinking water from the Creek of Madness, which explained why some of the unworthy were insane, why they had mental disorders, like Mariel, and it was said the Chosen didn't have gifts, that they weren't special, just disturbed. I know why they said all this.

A long time ago (without the Superior Sister knowing), we went into the Creek of Madness. It was a hot day, the sun was burning our skin, and a group of us wanted to cool down. All I did was dip my feet in and wet my face and hair, but some risked dunking their whole bodies. It's quite shallow, so they lay in the water, let it flow over them, to feel the cool relief of the current against their skin. Catalina made the mistake of opening her mouth. When they got out and we were drying off, she clutched her head. At first she didn't say anything, just pressed her hands to her temples and opened her eyes. We're forbidden from going into the creek; we had to get back before anyone found out. I stood and shook her, tried to get her to react. Finally, she spoke: Spiders are crawling through my thoughts. I feel the tips of their legs like hot pins pricking my brain very slowly. She didn't scream when she said this, just repeated it until she fainted. Now no one claims we're given water from the creek; the Superior Sister herself made sure to eradicate that rumor. Nor does she allow us to see the crickets we eat with gratitude and resignation. We don't see them, but the chirping is an indestructible hum that racks our bodies, sharp and penetrating.

I looked at the glass of water on the table. The candle's light was weak, but I thought I saw a strange movement in the water, like something in it was alive.

(Could it be water from the Creek of Madness?

Could I be mad?

Deranged?

Insane?)

Before I lay down, before I fell asleep for a few minutes, I remembered the quartz in the pocket of my tunic. I took it out and saw a black, opaque stone. I had to hold back a furious scream.

Atrocious, insidious Lourdes had replaced the stone when she'd left the Minor Saint in the Tower of Silence. I still don't understand how I could have been so stupid, so gullible. How I didn't realize that Lourdes would never have let a treasure like the quartz be trapped in the hands of a corpse.

I wanted ~~to kill her,~~ I want ~~to kill her.~~ I want ~~to tie her up,~~ I want ~~to strike her,~~ I want ~~to destroy her,~~ I want ~~to break her,~~ I want ~~to lick her,~~ I want ~~to take off her clothes,~~ I want ~~to torture her,~~ I want ~~to kill her, kill her, kill her.~~ I want

*   *   *

Mom said there'd never been a good year while she was alive. Her great-grandparents had been the last to experience a sense of well-being. She had always lived with ecological disasters, which worsened day by day. At least we can still feed ourselves, she told me, live in peace at home. Our home where swallows nested in the roof. Mom believed that swallows only nested in happy homes. How do they know, Mom? How can they tell a happy home from a sad one? Because there's a brilliance to happy people. It expands and things become imbued with it. What does imbued mean? That the light lingers on what they touch. The swallows can see it.

Maybe I'm idealizing my memories. Maybe they're fictions I want to believe. My mother let herself die on the kitchen floor, of hunger, of sadness, of exhaustion. I don't blame her for abandoning me.

At the House of the Sacred Sisterhood there are no swallows. We can't tell the seasons apart; in a single week, all four might merge together, one crossing over into another, destroying it, the cold of winter freezing a spring day, the heat melting autumnal peace, each season surrounded by a piercing silence that spreads with increasing speed. The silence of birds that rarely sing anymore.

Someone from the Sacred Sisterhood tried to circulate the forbidden calendar year. But the Superior Sister also destroyed that rumor with lashings. We don't know what year it is. I hope that if someone is reading these pages, they live in a world where time is measured artificially, even though we know it's a construction, even though we intuit that behind the numerical structure, there's nothing other than right now. Maybe in some future place it'll be YEAR ONE again, or maybe it'll be the YEAR OF THE RED DRAGON, and people will no longer use numbers, they'll use beautiful words like the YEAR OF THE FIRE-FLIES, the YEAR OF THE INVISIBLE WOLF. What about the Chinese calendar—what year is it? And the Hebrew cal-endar? Why do I care so much if time and space disappear when the world has come undone? Will there be borders and countries again in the future? Today, here, right now, the days don't matter. Or the months. They disappear like sand between my fingers, without a trace. Except in this book of the night, in this clandestine calendar, where this day could be called the DAY OF THE DEER.

After I'd brought her food and water in the Tower of Silence, where she'd kept hidden as I'd asked, after one of the servants had found the body of a wanderer who'd fainted in the garden (which is what I'd told her to do, pretend she'd fainted, say she didn't remember how she'd gotten there), after the servant ran to let the others know, and the bell was rung, after another servant tossed water on her

from a distance, and she pretended to wake, uncomprehending, after we told her to keep a distance and led her
to the Cloister of Purification, after her quarantine there,
after a servant, teary-eyed and apprehensive (afraid she'd
catch something), gave her food and drink (enforced by
the Superior Sister's whip), after it was confirmed that
she showed no signs of contamination, after the Superior
Sister announced she could join us, only then was she to
be officially welcomed to the Sacred Sisterhood.

Today, the DAY OF THE DEER, her day, they're going
to assign her a cell and a name. Today they'll give her a
clean tunic and remove her stained dress and combat
boots. Today the sun is still high and I write isolated in my
windowless cell, by the sliver of light that enters through
the crack, through the fissure I've chipped at carefully,
diligently, through the crevice that allows me to breathe.
I write while I wait for the bells to ring and announce the
beginning of the ceremony.

It's been a while since so clear a candidate for Chosen
or Enlightened has appeared. That's why the House of the
Sacred Sisterhood is like a wasp's nest. The chirping of
the crickets mixes with the subterranean hum of uneasy
voices, lying in wait.

*   *   *

The deer is now called Lucía.

*   *   *

He told us that to be Enlightened, we had to cease being irascible flowers, scorpions teeming with venom, bloated with poison, beasts with pointed tails, scattering apathy and depravity, causing the whole world to reek. We looked at María de las Soledades, who hunched her shoulders and lowered her head. She no longer spoke words. She'd lost them all. One of the wounds from the spiked cilice had gotten infected. María de las Soledades covered her mouth with her hand, but day by day we saw her lips deform, saw them swell, festering with a whitish color. The stigma of disgrace.

With her black boots, the Superior Sister struck the light wood floor. Her steps were almost inaudible, but I could detect them. Steps like jabs. Her leather whip hung down to her feet, her special whip. The stained glass was opaque because there were clouds in the sky. The white deer looked dark, blurred. He threatened us with an incessant rain of fire and burning sand. He was behind the chancel screen, as always, and though His voice was a black wave that could fossilize blood, our impure blood, I heard it from a distance, like an echo lost in a cave, because

I couldn't help but feel Lucía's presence. She was by my side and trusted me. We shared a secret; we're united by loyalty.

I touched the rough cloth of her tunic with my finger. I felt the abyss of her scent, her skin suffused with a blue paradise that I wanted to set myself free in, let myself go in, fall into forever. I struggled to concentrate because Lucía radiated something else. Longing? No, she wasn't burdened by the many-headed serpent of desire. I was bloated with avarice. We all were. The servants wanted to stop serving, though they couldn't, though they would go on being who they were for the rest of their lives. We unworthy wanted to stop being unworthy so we could be Chosen (mutilated) or Enlightened. We could be emissaries of the light if we made enough sacrifices. Though there was not much evidence of this desire. We struggled to adapt, to understand. Some didn't even speak the House of the Sacred Sisterhood's language. But it wasn't avarice in Lucía's case. She had the certainty of those who know what they're doing because they think things through, because they strategize, or simply because they understand they're special.

As though she knew what to do, as though someone had instructed her in the practices and ways of the Sacred Sisterhood, Lucía impressed the Superior Sister during the renaming ceremony. She was submissive, diligent, grateful, open to what she was receiving. Disciplined.

She got down on her knees before she was told, kept her head lowered at all times, accepted her name as though it had always been hers. Her meekness was perfection. Throughout the ceremony, Lourdes looked at her with an unhinged smile. We all looked at Lucía suspiciously, uneasily. At that moment, I knew the others would hurt Lucía, that they would not allow her to be a candidate for Chosen or Enlightened. But I also knew, at that moment, at that exact moment, and I know it now as I write in the red ink of poisonous berries, that I will protect her, even if she is a rival, even if I too want to be Enlightened. I want to feel that paradise as often as I can.

And no one is going to take it from me.

*　　　*　　　*

Circe. The sorceress.

I saw the sparkle in her yellow eyes when I fled the city so the adults wouldn't find me. I had my knife, my hunger, and my thirst.

I can't write about Circe, not yet, because she took part of my light, the light I need to run through my veins again.

To purify.

*　　　*　　　*

The sky has been dirty for days, the color of mud. There are black clouds in it that seem static. Their stillness is making us nervous. Ever since we welcomed Lucía it's seemed like rain was coming, like a storm was approaching, but it hasn't happened. The Enlightened declared it would be acid rain. The Superior Sister ordered the servants to shelter the animals (which we've never seen, not near the crops, not in a corral—do they even exist?). She told them to cover up the few crops we have. (What's the point of covering up the crops? The tainted water penetrates the pores of the earth and seeps down into their roots.)

The acid rain is dangerous. It burns.

That's what the others murmur, that it can incinerate us from the inside, char our blood, but ever since I arrived, the rain has always been water falling from the sky, water we collect and save like liquid gold. No one can explain how and why acid rain still exists if the factories have stopped operating, if there are fewer and fewer humans. But the Superior Sister insists it does and she knows because the Chosen and Enlightened have confirmed it. They say that after she migrated, like so many others driven from their inhospitable countries by tornadoes, drought, and famine, she moved with the millenary tribes, tribes of sage women who taught her to live without depending on civilization, far before the collapse. Because these women knew how to read the signs. They also say the Superior Sister fought in the water wars, the most violent ones, in which the millenary tribes were bombarded, and that she defended her own until the very end, that she was a prisoner, a slave, that she escaped. We have no way of confirming any of this, but we believe it all because the Superior Sister carries the story of her life with her, in every step she takes, it's there, the excess, we feel it, and that's why we fear and admire her.

The Superior Sister announced that the unworthy had to make a sacrifice. That we needed to preserve the purity of our space, to keep the delicate balance from exploding, to save the House of the Sacred Sisterhood from contamination, and to ensure that God averts the acid rain. "Without faith, there is no refuge," she repeated, and rang her small bell several times. The Full Auras saw the signs in the sky. The Diaphanous Spirits heard them in the buzzing of the insects, in the slightest shift of the clouds, in the plants' growth. The Minor Saints warned us with celestial song, and the Enlightened, the emissaries of the light, declared it to be acid rain.

This is a test, shouted the Superior Sister. Another test from which we will emerge victorious. ~~But I didn't quite believe her this time, because her bell kept ringing, as though by moving it she could cast some sort of spell to stop the acid rain from threatening us.~~

Lourdes stood up. We looked at her, certain she would have the best idea, the best sacrifice of all time. But before she could open her mouth, Lucía did, and in her yellow voice, with her wolfish words, she said: I offer to walk on burning embers.

The small bell stopped ringing suddenly.

Lucía smiled.

We looked at her in silence, incredulous. She didn't seem to be aware of anything, or maybe she was and simply didn't care. She didn't register Lourdes's pursed lips, her clenched fists wrinkling her tunic, which was always impeccable. Nor that the Superior Sister was still, like a broken stone sculpture. No one had ever offered to make a sacrifice of that magnitude. When the Superior Sister demands an impossible sacrifice of us, we nominate one of the weak, an unworthy due some punishment. The servants aren't worthy of sacrifice. We think it's unfair, but we understand we can't accept blood as contaminated as theirs. No one moved. Then Lucía went up to the Superior Sister and got down on her knees. She was beautiful, but hers was a new, unsettling beauty. At the time, I couldn't say why. Only that I felt uncomfortable when I looked at her, as though my body were suddenly foreign. Then I understood. She was the maker of an entire universe, an inner universe, her own, and she was the sole inhabitant.

The Superior Sister looked disconcerted, seeking a response. She stammered and put one of her hands, so delicate and strong, on Lucía's head. She said: "Tonight." Then she rang her bell and ordered the servants to ready every aspect of the sacrifice.

Lucía rose with an intense serenity, without smiling or boasting, as though she truly believed her sacrifice would change something.

The servants prepared the path of embers near the wall. We waited in our cells until the bells tolled. Thick air entered through the crevice in my wall. We put on our veils and crossed the garden. He was in the tower, or so we believed. The black clouds were static, as though the sky were an enormous canvas bearing the catastrophe. The haze was dense and we struggled to breathe. It felt like we could touch the water in the air. Our veils stuck to our skin, our tunics were stifling, but I felt a chill inside me that crept along my bones.

We heard a clap of thunder. We trembled, though there was no wind.

Lucía appeared, guarded by three of the unworthy. She had on a white tunic, her loose hair adorned with dry leaves. They were red and orange. I saw her as I had the first time in the ~~woods~~ space full of trees, saw the magnificence and fragility of a deer, the helplessness that moves you to protect her from the world, from herself, but she wasn't there, not entirely, because she was walking in a trance. I'd tried to go to her cell before the sacrifice, I'd wanted to calm her down, reassure her that I would treat her wounds, feed her, take care of her. But I didn't because I heard the Superior Sister's boots in the hallway, monitoring us.

When Lucía walked by me, I smelled her scent, that paradise on the verge of igniting, and I looked at her anxiously. But it was as though what was about to happen, the act that she herself had brought on, was a distant dream, another's dream.

I held out my hand to touch her, sought the slightest contact, but all I felt was the coarse cloth of one of the unworthy's tunics, the heavy tunics we wear every day.

The Superior Sister rang her bell and the unworthy led Lucía to the path of embers. For a second, we didn't know what to do and we looked at each other through the veils that make it hard to breathe. We all wondered silently how to proceed with this kind of sacrifice. The Superior Sister rang her bell again and Lourdes was the first to get down on her knees and recite: Without faith, there is no refuge. The rest of us followed suit and I felt the dense humidity of the sky on my back. The invisible burden. We breathed hot particles and again and again, we repeated: Without faith, there is no refuge.

Behind the clouds we saw lights appear and disappear, the lightning held by the black sky. A catastrophe can contain such beauty, I thought.

The Superior Sister rang her bell and we all went quiet. She approached Lucía and put a hand on her shoulder. Then she whispered something in her ear. Lucía nodded and took the first step, her feet bare and spotless, as though she hadn't walked through the grass and earth in the garden, as though she'd levitated there.

One of the leaves decorating her hair fell onto the embers and we saw it go up in flames.

The smell of fire was weak because of the humidity, which threatened to put the embers out, but I could sense them gaining strength. The chirping of the crickets intensified, and we heard a bird's song. Fleeting but beautiful. It moved us. Maybe it was the same bird that sang the night I found the white deer.

In the dark evening light, we saw the embers crackle. They seemed alive, one color changing into another. Red, orange, white. The colors vanished and then returned, as though the heat were transmitting a hidden message in the secret language of fire. Lucía walked on those words of light, walked without showing pain, walked slowly, almost as if she were dancing, walked as if she alone were witnessing the miracle. When she reached the other side she stopped but didn't smile. She looked at us, and I felt she was seeing us for the first time. She closed her eyes and knelt down in the earth. Her feet didn't have a single burn on them. They were clean. We all held our breath. Some covered their mouths with both hands. At the time, I even thought the crickets had stopped chirping, as though they had intuited what had happened.

Commotion.

The Superior Sister's bell dropped to the earth and the sound was hollow, the empty sound of something that has broken forever. She stared at Lucía, her mouth ajar, that mouth of hers that's always a little red. She moved her hands slightly, as though she didn't know what to do with them.

I looked toward the tower. He, or the silhouette we believed to be Him, remained there, motionless.

We returned to our cells without understanding, perplexed. Some whispered that the servants had seen Lucía put something on her feet, others that the fire had been very difficult to light, and the embers weak, because of the excess humidity. Another explained that it all depended on control of the mind, but nobody paid her any attention. Lourdes said nothing, she just walked rigidly, in silence. Her fists were closed, tightly clenched.

I don't understand either, as I write now, as I ask myself who I helped. Who is she? Am I willing to do anything for a stranger?

Lucía, immune to fire.

* * *

Today dawned cloudless, but we couldn't enjoy the relief or celebrate the sacrifice's success because we heard screams coming from the cells.

I ran through the hallways, we all did; we ran until we reached Lucía's cell, but what happened was confusing and it was over fast. I tried to enter her cell but couldn't, the unworthy were blocking the door. I thought the worst, pushed them aside, elbowed them in the ribs, but they were completely still as they looked on, silent. They wouldn't let me pass. Afterward some said it had seemed impossible, as though a dream had materialized at that moment, a dream verging on a nightmare. All I heard was someone screaming, her cries rhythmic, deliberate, as though her breathing were part of an endless wail. Later I was told it had been Lourdes.

The unworthy saw Lucía surrounded by wasps. They saw the perfect hexagonal cells of the wasps' nest lying on the floor. Broken. Split in two. They figured Lourdes had forced some of the unworthy to look for it in the place they call the ~~woods~~, to put it in Lucía's bed during the night.

Some say that Lucía, her black hair falling onto her white nightgown, looked like a living sculpture. At first they thought her eyes were closed, but they were fixed on the floor. The black-and-yellow wasps had surrounded her, but they did not attack. Instead they hovered there, like they were waiting for orders. They had formed an aura around her. An aura that seemed to pulse. She was crowned by a cloak of wasps. No one spoke; we just listened to Lourdes's wailing and the sharpened buzzing, the damage lurking in the air. The fury.

Some believe they saw Lucía raise her eyes very slowly, and then the wasps stop buzzing. No one could explain it clearly, but they said the wasps began to scream with their bodies. Those who were there said the screaming, which seemed human, was emitted by the body of each wasp vibrating violently. A group broke off from the swarm to attack Lourdes. Lucía looked to one side and the rest of the wasps flew toward some of the unworthy, Lourdes's weaklings, though no one can say for sure because they all fled screaming, desperate. That I did see, the moment some of the weaklings fell to the floor and others climbed over them, trampling heads, backs, hands, legs.

As they were running away I stepped into an empty cell, and when they were gone, I went to look for Lucía. I found her standing there in silence, her head held high, a slight smile on her face. I wrapped my arms around her. I don't know if seconds passed, or hours, or minutes, all I know is that at one point she took my face in her hands and stroked my cheek. Then she stepped back and looked at the nest. I knelt down and very carefully picked up the two pieces. They were rough to the touch, like ancient paper, and I remembered my mother asking me why bees and wasps built their honeycombs, their nests, like they did. She had drawn a hexagon on a piece of paper and a question mark in the middle of it. She did things like that sometimes, encouraged me to think. It took hours, maybe days, before I finally answered that nature doesn't make mistakes, that the structure had to be the best one to keep the honeycomb strong. I didn't say the word structure, I said something more basic, like: Its shape. She interrupted me: It's called a hexagonal shape. Okay, Mom, I said, the hexagonal shape makes the bees' and wasps' houses strong. She gave me a kiss on the nose and said: That's it, my beautiful girl, you got it. And it also allows them to store honey better. All of this I remembered in the seconds or milliseconds it took me to pick up the nest and give the pieces to Lucía, who looked at me silently as I fell into the paradise she was, as I surrendered.

Without saying a word, she walked barefoot to the garden. I followed. I tried to cover her with a sheet because all she had on was her nightgown, which was translucent in the morning sun, in the sun that now shone on us, thanks to her. She ignored me and kept walking.

A Diaphanous Spirit in the garden heard her light steps. She stopped turning in circles, her right palm no longer open to the sky, nor her left to the earth, lowered her arms and stood still to listen carefully. I had to close my eyes for a second because the sacred crystal that hung from her neck reflected the sun, and I was blinded by the gleam of light. The Diaphanous Spirit looked at Lucía and smiled. Diaphanous Spirits never smile. Ever. They hate us, they want us to suffer, to be aware of the black holes, the abominable caverns that are their tongueless mouths, which they open so we see the darkness. But this Diaphanous Spirit smiled as though she knew something, as though in Lucía's steps she had grasped certain truths. When she heard me, when she realized the soft steps in the grass were mine, when she saw me from afar, she stopped smiling. But I kept looking at her, like I always do with Diaphanous Spirits. Challenging her.

The wasps punished those responsible, stabbing them with their retractable stingers again and again, possibly biting them, black jaws on arms, eyes, feet, mouths;

then they followed Lucía. Or that's what I think I saw. Her black hair shone in the sun and what looked like golden, transparent wings gave off tiny glints of light. When Lucía reached the end of the garden, she and what were likely the wasps entered the thicket. I wanted to go up to her, to go with her, but she turned around and looked at me in such a way that I understood I was to stay there, that I would be excluded from the pulsing, green tangle and remain far from the shrill aura that had formed around her again.

Lucía, wasp charmer.

During breakfast, the Superior Sister said nothing. She observed us from her chair. The whip lay motionless on the floor. She seemed to be enjoying the spectacle. Lourdes and her minions waited in silence, their heads lowered so we wouldn't see their swollen eyes, their deformed mouths. But we noticed the marks, the shame, the rage, the dismay. Perfectly well. They hid their hands, writhed in pain.

Lucía was on time and sat down next to me. She was clean, showed no sign of having walked among the trees, gotten dirt on herself, sweated under the morning sun. She had no stings of any kind. The servants brought us breakfast and the Superior Sister a mug. This was strange, she didn't eat or drink in our presence. With the mug in her hand, she stood and went over to Lucía. She placed it on the table, next to the mushy mixture we eat in the morning that tastes of crickets. The Superior Sister was silent as she looked at Lucía, then she touched her briefly on the shoulder. I could smell the coffee. Lucía took the mug and inhaled the aroma, but before taking a sip, she gave Lourdes a long look without saying a word.

I felt pleasure at seeing Lourdes defeated. I felt

*　　　*　　　*

I felt like crying again. But I didn't, not there, not with Lucía triumphant, not with Lourdes on the verge of a nervous breakdown, which she tried to hide and hold in, though I knew her well enough to recognize the pursed lips, the white fists, the staring, glassy eyes, as rage, that dragon that burns inside you. I too hid what I was feeling and smiled, because in my thoughts all I saw was Circe. But I didn't cry, not there; I wasn't going to share my personal misfortune, my intimate pain. Not with these women whom the wasps had stung, wounded, filled with venom.

*　　　*　　　*

Circe. My Circe. My sorceress. The first thing I saw was her eyes. She was as terrified as I was, and I saw her fear in those two borderless universes that looked at me without blinking. I thought she was going to attack so I grabbed my knife. But I didn't try to scare her off or hurt her, because I had no strength left. I was tired of escaping, I'd been walking for days, distancing myself from the city and the murderous adults. I was cold, thirsty, hungry, and all I wanted was to sleep in the abandoned building I'd found, in the ruined cathedral, its stained glass windows broken by the branches of dead trees that had stopped growing long before.

Without taking my eyes off her, my knife pointed at her head, I walked slowly toward the confessional, a replica in miniature of what the cathedral once was, careful not to trip on the rubble. I'd never been in a building like it, but I knew the difference between a chapel, a church, and a cathedral. My mother had shown me books on Gothic architecture. She loved the ribs, the pinnacles, the steeples, the archivolts. The books had images of buildings that no longer existed. The Notre-Dame Cathedral had burned down, the Chartres Cathedral had been sacked and destroyed in multiple wars, Westminster Abbey and York Minster were underwater, like all of what was once the United Kingdom. My mother would touch the images in the books and ask herself over and over how something so beautiful could disappear.

I opened the door to the confessional and sat down on a bench, the cushion dirty but comfortable. From there I could keep watch over Circe, see her through the holes in the carved wooden door, which I'd closed slowly. She didn't try to attack either, just gave me a long, distrusting look, until at some point we both fell asleep on our respective watches.

The next day, when I woke, I opened the door cautiously and saw Circe watching me. I wondered why she hadn't escaped, what was keeping her there. Had I invaded her home? Should I feel like an intruder? My whole body hurt from the tension, cold, and hunger. I missed the tarantula kids, my small family of piranhas. I'd gotten used to surviving with them, needed their silent laughter, the strategies thought up by Ulysses, who'd been born to be the leader we admired and loved. He wasn't much bigger than the rest of us, but he knew what was essential to survive. His mother and father, who'd fought in the water wars, had trained him well. When I asked him what he knew of those wars he said, not much, that his mother hadn't wanted to talk about them, because people she'd loved had lost their lives. His father hadn't told him anything either. When Ulysses asked his mother if she'd killed anyone, an enemy, she looked at him silently for several minutes, and he saw her eyes harden as she tried to hold back tears. There were no enemies, she told Ulysses, only people trying to survive, people dying of thirst and hunger. None of us could bring ourselves to ask him what had happened to his parents, where they were now, because when he stopped speaking, he lowered his head, sighed, and went to sleep.

I got up very carefully, without making any sudden movements. I took a few steps, and when I looked down, I saw an enormous cross split in two, its wood rotten. There was a stained glass window up high that wasn't broken, the light of the sun filtering through it. Blues and greens predominated, but I couldn't appreciate its beauty. One of the trees that had fallen and broken part of the stained glass looked like an ancient skeleton. I didn't think this at the time, just intuited it, and I would have been unable to put it into words, but I saw solitude in all its dimensions there, in the lack of vegetation on the walls, on the floor, covering what had been created by human hands. Nowhere did I see nature, unstoppable, free, spreading; there was just a dead tree.

I wasn't going to find food there.

Suddenly I heard a warble. I was startled. It had been a while since I'd seen a pigeon. We'd hunted the few we saw in the city with slingshots. Ulysses had the best aim, though mine was pretty good too, almost as good as his. Now my slingshot was in the backpack I had left with the tarantula kids. When I found them dead, when I said goodbye to my friends, when I couldn't cry, I left my backpack behind to buy time so the adults would look through it, so they'd share the bounty and I could survive. I had to run, be light on my feet, and I couldn't carry the weight. All I took was the knife I always kept in my belt. I was never without it. Ulysses had taught me that, like so many things, like how to use a slingshot to hunt or to harm. He had found me, filthy, malnourished, weak, and had taken me into his small family, a group of piranha kids who could pick the locks on doors and windows, find food in the most unlikely places, treat each other's wounds, take care of each other. That's why the adults hated us, because we didn't need them, because day by day we grew stronger. We were the competition. That's why they killed my small family of beautiful kids.

This yellow page, this piece of paper that has resisted time, now has splotches on it from my tears. I tried to hold them back so the ochre ink wouldn't run. But I couldn't. It hurts to write about the tarantula kids, that's why I didn't remember them, why my mind had emptied before I came to the House of the Sacred Sisterhood.

I considered using wood from the fallen cross for a makeshift slingshot, in case there were more birds or rats. Then I heard a brief, agonized squawk and saw Circe with the bloody pigeon in her mouth. I thought about stealing it from her, but that would have been dangerous.

I returned to the wooden receptacle, to what looked like a miniature house, a useless house. I left the door open to observe Circe from a place of apparent protection. I saw her chew and destroy the pigeon, its tiny body that nevertheless had enough meat. Two bites could stave off hunger. She watched me as she ate, with those eyes like constellations, like an ocean of sparkling, expectant stars. I was a predator to her, a potential threat. She had reason to fear me. After all, I was a tarantula kid, a piranha kid, a scorpion kid, a serpent kid.

I ached with hunger, it struck at me, like when I'd first met my family of crazy kids and didn't want to hunt abandoned pets. I knew I wasn't going to hunt Circe, that I wouldn't run the risk of her attacking me. I tried to focus on a strategy, plan what to do next, think what Ulysses would have done, where to go, how to continue, but I couldn't reason. Hunger was consuming my thoughts, clouding my vision. That's why I didn't see Circe slowly approaching the confessional. I was watching her, but I didn't see her.

*   *   *

The ink I write in now is black. I made it with charcoal I stole from the servants. I'm in my cell and it's very late, but I have time. The moonlight coming through the crack lets me see these dark words with complete clarity.

The silence here, the silence at the House of the Sacred Sisterhood, is like a white serpent slithering through the air, curling up in the void.

Circe would never have done me harm, though I didn't know it at the time. I grabbed my knife but didn't attack, because she left a piece of pigeon on the confessional's step. An offering. It wasn't much, but it warranted a fire. I'd cook the meat over pieces of the cross that weren't rotten. Circe climbed into one of the broken window frames and watched the whole process from up there. She saw me wrap my hands in the strips of fabric I kept around my neck for that very purpose, so I wouldn't get splinters when I found wood. The tarantula kids had taught me how to make fire with almost anything, under any circumstances. I knew that eating uncooked meat was risky, and also that I could endure hours and days of fasting. If you did things wrong it could kill you. Succumbing to anxiety was dangerous.

Circe was alert to each of my movements. I walked through the cathedral, among the debris, stepping on an angel's wings by mistake, the sculpture broken on the floor. Some of the pews were whole, but the wood had markings in it, drawings and sentences. Other pews seemed to have been taken apart, the planks scattered on the floor. One was the ideal shape and thickness to make fire, and I moved it off to the side. I kept walking and saw a headless sculpture.

It looked like a woman because of the folds in its tunic, carved in stone, and its large, delicate hands.

Close to the sculpture of the decapitated woman—a saint? a martyr? a virgin?—I found a dry stick I could rub against the hardwood plank to make fire. The sculpture of the woman was on a marble pedestal. The pedestal had a locked door that no one had been able to pick. But I knew how, and I easily opened the door with my knife. Inside there were empty vases and small metal bowls. I'd use them to boil the water in the baptismal font. I figured it was rainwater, because the roof above it was broken. The roof was incredibly high, unreachable. It had been blue, and there were small golden stars painted on it that no longer shone.

A bit farther into the cathedral I saw ribs that formed a huge flowery panel in the central cupola. Veins of stone that had resisted time, humans, and catastrophes. It was one of the few parts of the roof that was still intact. The cupola protected what had been the main altar, which was missing the cross rotting on the floor. To the right of the altar I saw an open door. I entered cautiously, but the room had been completely sacked, there was no furniture, no objects, no glass in the windows, and one of the walls was gone, a wall that had likely bordered a larger room, of which only the columns and pillars remained.

I returned to the baptismal font and collected water. I knew I had to boil the water before drinking it. The heat would kill any viruses, parasites, bacteria. As I waited for the water to settle in the bowls, I shaved wood to start the fire. I gathered branches that had fallen from the dead tree, enough to keep the fire going for a while. I cleaned and cooked the bit of meat that Circe had given me, and boiled and drank the baptismal water. I relieved my dry throat and staved off hunger. I smiled. I'm not sure if that was happiness, but it was something like it.

When she saw the fire, Circe got down from the window. She kept a prudent distance, though she knew she had as much right to the fire as I did. She positioned herself precisely where she could feel the heat and still be able to escape if I were to attack. I let some time pass, then approached with measured movements and left her one of the bowls of water.

My offering.

First she sniffed at the water, and then she drank it, looking at me cautiously the whole time. But by that point we knew we could trust each other. No one feeds someone they're going to kill. The stars that made up the constellations in her eyes began to sparkle. We slept by the fire.

The next day I went through the cathedral again. Circe followed me, curious, but still at a distance. Under some planks we found a piece of red cloth, a rusty red. I tied it to my body like a backpack. In it I put the bowls I'd cook with. The night before I'd filled a small vase with the left-over baptismal water I'd boiled. The vase in one hand and the stick I'd used to make fire in the other, I left the cathedral with Circe.

*　　　*　　　*

It's been days since I've written, unable to touch these pages, days of anxiety, as though a sickness were spreading through my veins, as though the words accumulating in my blood were secreting venom, a toxic substance, an acid forcing me to let them out.

They burn and it's as though a desert of words were forming inside me, words converting into hot, dry sand, decomposing into scorching particles.

While I was writing about the tarantula kids and Circe, I was almost discovered. It was Lucía who entered my cell unannounced, after opening the door suddenly, and the only thing that saved this secret book of the night was the candle's flame going out. The night was pitch-black, only darkness entered through the crevice in the wall, along with a weak, warm breeze that didn't put out the flame. It was Lucía's untimely entry that snuffed it out, giving me time to hide these painful memories.

(Words that are forbidden)

(Words with sharp edges)

(Words of fire)

I asked how she wasn't seen, how it could be possible, because the Superior Sister monitors the hallways at that hour. Lucía smiled and said: When I want to be, I'm invisible. I think my eyes widened and my jaw dropped because she laughed, and said: Don't worry, I was very careful, no one saw me. Then she asked me to meet her in the garden later, said she had to talk to me. It was already night and we were not supposed to go out. But I said yes because I knew what she wanted to talk about.

The rumor began a few days after the miracle of the wasps, as some referred to it. Others said (whispered) that nothing had happened according to the rumor, that Lucía didn't have powers of any kind, that everyone's perception had been altered by their fear of the wasps. But Lourdes and her disciples began to call Lucía a witch, a lover of demons, a maleficent woman, a devourer of souls, a queen of the dark. They whisper the rumor in the hallways, they insinuate it, they enter her cell and stain her sheets with black earth and blood, leave behind figures of dry branches bound with thread, smeared with feces. They go quiet when she appears, lower their heads, refuse to look her in the eye.

Before I left my cell and walked through the hallways, I made sure the silence was total. That I was alone. Stealthily, I found my way to the black door of carved wood. I rested my head against it and didn't hear anything for a long while, nothing that would reveal the presence of the Enlightened. (What is it like to hear the words emitted by the mouth of God? Are they small, ephemeral explosions? Does his tongue cradle death?)

God is hungry.

Someone screamed on the other side of the door. It was like a shrill cry, cutting. A wail? One of the Enlightened trying to chew shards of glass? I was startled.

~~It was then that I asked myself why I wanted to be Enlightened. Did I really want to be an emissary of the light? To live locked up? To be an intermediary between God and this contaminated world? Was my~~ help ~~neces-sary, my participation? Escaping from the House of the Sacred Sisterhood means death in the devastated lands. Are the miracles in this blessed space real? Or is it the water in the Creek of Madness that causes us to believe? To question means living in the desert. In a heaven with no~~ God?

Another scream behind the door. A stifled scream, a scream not meant to be heard. I took off at a run.

I found Lucía at the edge of the garden, where ~~the woods~~ the thicket begins. The night was pitch-black. I saw her looking at the sky, her arms raised, and I saw the dense clouds shift to reveal the full moon, and in her stillness, her icy beauty was clear, the beauty I had seen the night we spoke for the first time. She was looking at the stars.

She was oblivious to it all, as though she were trapped in the intangible dimension, in that place beyond the air where the Superior Sister says the Chosen go, the ones we never see again. Some say these Chosen detect dark messages, confuse the true signs from our God with those of the erroneous God, the false son, and the negative mother. Lucía's body was present, her sweet smell, the blue abyss, but she was not there.

I went over to her. She didn't hear my steps, so I spoke. I said: Lucía, here I am. Her gaze remained lost in the sky, absorbing the white energy of the moon, the funereal radiance of the stars. I touched her very slowly with my fingertips, fearful that her snowy beauty would burn me. But she smiled, took my hand, and we entered the thicket.

*   *   *

How can I write what happens next? If someone finds these pages, the Superior Sister will break my fingers, yank out my eyes, lash me to obliteration. She'll see to it that I die suffering new pain, atone with my blood. That's why I tore and burned the pages that came before these, those that spoke of she who is below the earth, her mouth open, the insurgent, the disobedient one, Helena. That's why I betrayed her. I told the others about the chain with the gold cross under her mattress. That's why they buried her alive. That's the very reason I began to write again, to run the risk, so I wouldn't forget her, so I could retain in these words, in this attempt at capturing a life, a moment, a world, her smell, a scent like a sweet poison, like a sacred fire.

The servants went through our cells again, but this time I didn't see it coming. There were no half smiles, no murmurs, or I didn't notice them, immersed as I was in what had happened with Lucía. The previous day I'd hidden this book of the night in the room with the cleaning supplies, under some wooden planks, though sometimes I hide it in my cell or close to my heart, held in place by the strip of fabric. There are more and more pages, with every passing day it's more dangerous, more difficult to find safe hiding spots. They almost caught me. The servants gave me a look of such contempt. It's because they never find anything in my cell and lose out on the pleasure of the Superior Sister's punishments. The same servant from the last inspection stood there looking at the crevice. After examining it closely, she glared at me, laughed in silence, and called the Superior Sister. With steps like explosions, she appeared, monumental, but she didn't care much about the crevice. She hit the servant on her toothless mouth and told her not to waste time with nonsense. I felt the servant's hateful look, but I couldn't see her because my eyes were on the floor, my head lowered, as is expected of us.

That's why they didn't find these pages in my cell. But in María de las Soledades's cell they found a crucifix made of mud. They told me she didn't cry when the servants took turns kicking her. She had stopped speaking weeks before. The infection in her mouth had healed miraculously, but it had deformed her face. The servants kicked her half-heartedly because there were no cries or tears, just a silent body. They broke the cross and shouted that for worshippers of the erroneous God, the false son, and the negative mother there existed only perdition. Some of the unworthy gathered to look at María de las Soledades, who had curled into a ball on the floor, but no one helped her up. We all left. Some spat on her. Except for Lucía. Lucía stroked her head, hoisted her up, and took her to bed.

That story was told the next day after breakfast, when we all saw two antennae poking out of María de las Soledades's bowl, then the dark red, almost black, body of a cockroach emerging from the lumpy, white mixture. María de las Soledades looked at it and simply went on eating. She didn't care if the cockroach was trying to move, to save itself, to escape the thick whiteness. Lourdes covered her mouth because she was laughing. Lucía took the bowl from María de las Soledades, grabbed one of the antennae with two fingers, and tossed the half-dead cockroach at Lourdes. No one moved, no one said anything. They all looked at Lucía with a mixture of awe and disgust. I didn't know what to do, what to feel, after what had happened with her in the trees. I was still trying to figure out if it had been a dream, an illusion.

After that, as well as a witch, Lucía was called a cockroach.

*   *   *

We entered the darkness, through the trees. Lucía led me by the hand, seeming to know the way, as though she were guided by the moonlight.

We went farther into the thicket, into the space where the untamed are buried.

Suddenly we stopped. Lucía was still as she looked at a nebulous speck of light. At first I thought we were going to sit down, but then I saw the speck move through the air. I thought I was delirious, that I'd been given water from the Creek of Madness. I could hardly believe I was seeing a firefly. Its golden light shone, then disappeared, then shone again, like a tiny heart of fire beating in the night. Our mouths were open, but neither of us said a thing.

I cried in silence because words can't capture a sacred moment. What to say when you're in the presence of some-thing majestic? No one had seen a firefly in decades. My mother had told me about them, because her father had told her about them, like a myth passed down through gen-erations. The pesticides wiped them out, my mother told me, which her father had told her, which her grandfather had told him. But there it was, tiny and powerful. I got down on my knees and Lucía did the same. We saw it fly into the night, glow among the black trees, until it disap-peared. It was then that Lucía took my face in her hands and kissed me.

No one had ever kissed me; no one had ever run their tongue over my neck, my lips, that slowly. I couldn't bring myself to touch her, fearing there was no return from the abyss, but she didn't care about my shock or my submission, she just raised my tunic and removed it. She was decisive and gentle.

She undressed me in the blind moonlight; she undressed me among the trees.

I'd never experienced the pleasure of another's skin; no one had left me breathless, panting, at their mercy, my will gone, having surrendered; I'd never closed my eyes to be vulnerable, open.

I raised Lucía's tunic to where her breasts began, and I kissed the white deer's stomach, the dark night.

I felt the softness of her long, black hair on my skin. She looked me in the eye as she stroked my back with the tips of her fingers and opened my mouth with her tongue. Her touch set off flares under my skin, and an electric current began to course through my body like a wildfire of

water

air

wind.

I took off her tunic and ran my tongue over her breasts and mouth, as slowly as she had. No one had made me tremble before Lucía; no one had nibbled at my inner thighs, softly, nibbles like caresses.

I inhaled her fierce and sweet smell, felt her blue paradise enrapture me, envelop me, I was tossed into the abyss. The pleasure of her touch tore me apart because she'd let me into her inner universe, because we'd blazed together and together had created beauty. It was then that I opened my eyes and saw the impossible: we were surrounded by thousands of fireflies, tiny golden lights pulsing in the night, dancing in the dark. Lucía grabbed me by the hair and brought her whole body to mine, all of her skin, all of her mouth. We closed our eyes to cry out in unison, to disappear into one another. When we opened them, the fireflies were no longer there. But the light was.

Our own.

*   *   *

I seriously considered burning these pages or ripping up my confession. But I no longer care if the Superior Sister takes pleasure in torturing me or if the unworthy despise me.

All I care about is Lucía.

We lay there naked, my head resting on her chest, listening to her heartbeat. We looked at the lattice of branches, the black sky and the stars.

The fireflies must have been one of your miracles, I told her. Like the wasps and the embers. How else could they have been possible? If the world has collapsed, then there's nothing alive outside this place.

As Lucía stroked my back, she spoke in her wolf's voice, her translucent yellow, golden voice that was like touching the heart of the sun. She whispered: The truth is a sphere. We never see it whole, in its entirety. It slips down our throats, through our thoughts.

She went on talking, very close to my mouth but without touching it: The truth is changeable, it contracts, implodes, it's powerful like a bullet. And it can be lethal.

I asked her why she was telling me this, but she put a finger to my lips and brought hers even closer, until they were almost touching mine: The truth, a sphere that also contains within it a lie that spins at a different rhythm, like a cog that seems broken, unnecessary, but is vital to the mechanism's functioning. The challenge is finding the lie within the sphere.

After that we were silent. Lucía stretched an arm toward the sky as though she wanted to touch the stars. We're daughters of the moon, she said. She kissed me and I didn't know how to respond. All I could do was look at her; all I could do was run the tips of my fingers over her skin, very slowly, trying to hold on to each second, wanting to trap the moment in my hands.

We dressed and it was then that I realized we were next to the tree with the hollow. Lit by the stars and the moon, which seemed closer and closer, I showed it to her, and she said it could be our secret place. Our clandestine place. She got into the hollow and motioned for me to join her. We were so close to each other; we barely fit. We kissed inside the tree, in the dark hollow that smelled of the night, of something secret, of something lurking, hidden. She hugged me and it felt like I was inside an ancestral temple, a cathedral of wood and sap.

Trees, plants, mushrooms, emit a sound, each has its own melody, she told me. I can hear that melody if I really focus. This tree's song is sad, a funereal cadence. But it's beautiful, very solemn, as though a whole life were throbbing in the earth.

Then we walked, holding hands, and saw that the sky was still black, and the stars still visible, but that little by little, light was beginning to appear. The golden hour. The air smelled like summer still protected by the cold of early spring, or behind the cold, a summer that's burgeoning, that promises to be defiant, its hidden presence ensuring we anticipate its arrival.

Or was that the smell of happiness?

We went back to our cells cautiously, hiding along the way.

*   *   *

Lucía awoke a new thirst in me.

At this moment, in this instant, like a revelation, I understand that my body will await the sound of her voice.

Forever.

And as I write this, the first light entering through the crack, I think about her words and am alarmed. I'm troubled by Lucía's capacity to hear sounds that are almost inaudible, to carry out miracles, or at least that's what the unworthy say. I'm terrified by the Superior Sister's increasingly obvious interest in her. Everything points to her being a candidate for Chosen or Enlightened, but it's too soon. No, they can't choose her now.

No, they can't.

No

N

*   *   *

He told us that to be Enlightened we had to cease being recipients of evil, depositories of lies, daughters of filth, enemies of decorum, that we had to cease being the great mistake of nature, the traitors of wisdom and virtue, the offspring of perdition, that we had to rid ourselves of the muck in our blood. I looked at the veins in my wrists and my only thought was how close the words muck and luck were, and then I remembered Circe.

My enchantress.

We left the cathedral and walked for days, for months, for years. We slept in abandoned cars, in empty houses. We didn't find furniture or food, just broken walls and windows. Many others had passed through before us. I picked the locks on doors, cooked pieces of rat, pigeon, the occasional squirrel. I dug up earth and didn't find anything. Dead worms. The earth was dry, malnourished, anemic, agonizing, empty. I shared the water I was able to boil with Circe, water that wasn't completely contaminated, water we found in abandoned places, places where others hadn't been able to pick the locks, water we collected when it rained. For many kilometers, we walked beneath a sun that burned us, and saw no one. People were dying of hunger, animals were dying of hunger. They had died of hunger, of thirst, died with useless tongues and open eyes, died of rage, died in the dry earth.

We walked for so many kilometers that we reached what used to be a beach. But there was no sea. In the hot sand we found the remains of marine animals, the shells of tortoises and crabs, the skeletons of seagulls and fish. Circe played for a while with an empty shell. My mother had told me you could hear the waves in a shell, but when Circe stopped playing, I brought it to my ear and heard nothing. I sat down to contemplate the endless beach that had become a desert. Though it was hot, I felt an icy breeze. It smelled of something beautiful and fresh, of salt and movement. Was it the sea? In the distance, a black ship had run aground long ago.

One day we entered a small town with just a few houses. We'd already explored other towns. We knew it was important to do this because we always found something, we were meticulous. In an old house, a mansion, I found a secret door in a bookshelf that, by then, held almost no books. Behind the door there was another room with a table covered in a red velvet cloth. On it was a box of carved wood. I picked the lock and found jewels in the box. Colored crystals that had once been very valuable. But I couldn't carry it. The crystals were heavy, beautiful, useless. There was also a bottle covered in dust. The label said it was wine. With my knife I was able to remove the cork, and when I took a sip I spat it out.

In this new town, the small town, the locks on the doors were broken. We knew the chance of finding something we could use was very unlikely, but we still went from house to house to see if there was some food, a tin can, a bottle of water. In one of the houses, the only one that was red, there were paintings on the walls, paintings of barefoot, dirty children, with large, tear-filled eyes and bits of bread in their hands. No one had touched them. I stood looking at them while Circe explored. I was silent, unable to move, because the sad, famished children had hypnotized me, paralyzed me. I wondered what kind of person would hang those paintings and look at them every day. At that moment, standing in that empty house full of useless images, all I felt was rage, horrible rage. I also felt disgust, but I didn't understand why. I began to shred the paintings with my knife, deforming each painting, each child with large, tear-filled eyes, while I cried and screamed incoherent words, screamed my exhaustion, cried because I didn't have a bit of bread, because no one was going to paint my reality and hang it on a wall. Circe had stopped exploring and was silent by my side, as though she understood my desolation.

We went out into the garden, or into what had been a garden and was now an arid space with dead trees. I needed to compose myself, to stop crying. I sat down on the ground. Circe climbed into a tree and pawed at a honeycomb hanging from one of the highest branches. Circe wasn't called Circe yet. She wasn't my sorceress yet. I stood up and yelled at her to get down, as though she would listen to me, as though she could understand anything I said. If she destroyed the honeycomb we could die, I knew that well because I'd read it to the tarantula kids, who'd asked me how many stings it took to kill a human. Five hundred stings could kill one kid, I told them. They didn't know how many stings made up five hundred, but I explained that a single honeycomb could have almost thirty thousand bees. It could kill all of us and still have many bees to sting many other kids.

Circe ignored me. The honeycomb fell and split in two, but there were no bees in it. I found honey in some of the cells and knew it was edible, because it never goes bad. I'd also read that to the tarantula kids, said it was an eternal food. What's eternal? they'd asked. Something that lasts forever, I answered, though afterward I wasn't sure. Because the world was dying, because the world could also disappear. But at the time, I didn't think it through the way I am now, as I write by the light of a candle that's burning down little by little, while outside the sky is black and it's raining. We're no longer afraid of the acid rain, because of Lucía's sacrifice, and because the Enlightened, the emissaries of the light, declared the rain harmless. Without faith, there is no refuge, they said. I hear the water strike the buckets that we and the servants placed in the garden.

That day, the lucky day Circe found honey, all I did was reflect. I couldn't arrive at a fully formed thought. With the tip of my knife I removed what little honey I could salvage, and first I gave some to Circe, who'd already come down from the tree, curious. We ate the honey, very careful not to waste any, because we didn't know when we'd eat again. Circe licked her portion from the tip of my knife. That's how much we'd come to trust each other. Sometimes I carried her in my arms or put her on my shoulders so she wouldn't get too tired, and to feel her close to me. Still hungry, but happy with the treat we'd eaten, eternal in its transience, we left to explore the rest of the town.

The door to one of the houses was locked. I was surprised because the town seemed empty. I had no trouble picking the lock with my knife. I entered the house, wary of noise, careful in case we ran into someone violent, some adult willing to kill. It was hot outside, so the cold house was all the more striking. Circe felt it too, she walked with her tail puffed up, baring her fangs, her fur standing on end, as though she knew there was something strange in that place, a threat lurking.

Like the rest of the houses we'd gone through, this one was dirty and empty, but we heard a persistent noise. It was like wood creaking. We entered a room with large windows that opened onto a space at the back where real trees had once lived. There was a metal tree there now, the first I'd seen in a long time. Only the rich had been able to buy them. They purified the air and were intended to replace the living trees that had died off. But they weren't of much use without electricity. Ulysses had told me he'd lived close to a place with a ~~metallic woods~~.

Now I know why I can't write that word.

~~Woo~~

~~Wood~~

~~Woods.~~

Now I remember what happened in a ~~metallic woods~~, remember it hazily, chaotically. The only thing that's really present is the pain. I can't write it yet. My tears are smudging the ink on these pages. Erasing the letters. I have to stop.

This hurts.

How can you excise pain that radiates through your body, that torments your blood, that clings to your bones?

*   *   *

But I want to tell what happened before that, what we saw in that room, who or what we saw.

The room was large and practically empty. The light that entered through the open windows allowed us to see a single chair. We felt an icy cold, a strange wind blowing from the center of that dead garden. The rocking chair was moving back

    and

        forth,

back

    and

        forth.

That was the insistent noise, a sound like a broken song.

Back

    and

        forth,

back

    and

        forth.

A sick song amplified by the blank walls.

Circe moved back, afraid, but I stepped closer. The first thing I saw was a woman, her eyes closed, who seemed to be nursing a baby wrapped in an animal skin, but then I looked closer. What was latched to her breast seemed to be a rat, it had the teeth and tail of a rat, but it was bigger. She was cradling it, this thing that was eating her. I moved back, covering my mouth because I didn't want to scream, I didn't want that thing to look at me. Circe approached slowly, prepared to attack, and the thing stopped eating and bared its teeth. Teeth stained with blood. I think it growled or made a noise like stifled laughter. The woman kept rocking with her eyes closed,

back

and

forth,

back

and

forth.

She began to sing a sorrowful song without opening her mouth, without looking at us, and she patted the animal on the head, the enormous rat with a white face and black ears, its snout too long, its teeth feeding on the woman's flesh. The thing was feeding on flesh, hot, burning flesh, it was consuming flesh, feeding on her, the thing. The thing, the animal, stopped feeding for a second and looked at us, enraged, ready to do us harm. Its eyes were completely black, and they sparkled as though they were made of glass. I grabbed Circe as best I could and ran.

Desperate, breathless, I escaped along the main road, the only road, a dirt road with no trees, Circe squirming in my arms, because she didn't like it when I grabbed her suddenly. Then I let her go and we walked to calm ourselves down, to get away from the horror, to try to understand what we'd seen.

We didn't leave the town, because we had to keep exploring. We needed food.

In another empty house, in the back patio, we found clothes hanging on a line. The sun and wind had worn them out. Put holes in them. The scraps moved like broken flags. The clothes were dirty from the dust and sporadic rain, burned by the acid rain. I hadn't seen clothes on a line in years because people no longer washed them, or they did less and less, to preserve water. But there were those who washed their dirty clothes in contaminated rivers or who hung them in the sun, to air them out, bleach them, or disinfect them.

I sat down to look at the scraps of colors. There was something calming about the constant rhythm, the melody of movement.

I thought about the woman, I thought about rescuing her, but there was no point. She was already lost in her delirium. The monstrous rat was killing her.

I wrapped my arms around my legs, tucked my head between them, and swayed back and forth. I needed to calm myself down, but I started to cry. I cried with furious tears. I cried because I was exhausted, because I was helpless; I cried remembering my mother's hugs and how badly I needed them.

It was then that Circe brought me an offering. She'd trapped a cockroach, and when she left it half-dead next to my legs, I almost screamed in disgust, but I covered my mouth. I didn't want to offend her, and I didn't want that thing, that animal, to hear me. We were many houses away, but I was still shaken by the woman. The cockroach twitched its legs, as though it were trembling.

When she saw I wasn't going to eat it, Circe played with the bug a little, and it tried to escape but didn't get very far. Eventually she tired of chasing it and ate it. That was when I thought of the name Circe. I remembered the fascinated looks on the tarantula kids' faces when I read them a story about a woman who made candies for her boyfriend, cockroach candies. I also remembered that my mother had told me about a sorceress who could turn men into animals. She was a daughter of the sun, my mother had said, and knew everything about magic potions. She also had knowledge of medicine. She lived in the ~~woods~~ and her house was surrounded by lions and wolves that protected her. I imagined her to be powerful, invincible. I want to be Circe; I want to be a sorceress, an enchant-ress, I told Mom, who laughed in that way of hers that was a discovery every time. When she laughed it was like the air around her, the whole house, the colors, the world, sparkled more intensely.

Circe looked at me with eyes like oceans of silent lights. Circe, the enchantress, I said to her. It was the first time she approached me, and, very slowly, she sat between my crossed legs. I kept still, unsure what to do. I didn't want to touch her, to scare her away. I moved my fingers toward her very slowly and petted her. Her body began to vibrate, an enchantress's magical sound, and at that moment, I felt we were a pack of two.

*   *   *

~~Woods~~.

~~Woods~~.

~~Metallic woods~~.

*   *   *

For days, these pages were under a floorboard, protected. For days, I haven't written.

For days, Lucía and I have been escaping at night, wearing our veils as a precaution in case anyone sees us, hiding in our tree, Lucía telling me about certain flowers, the sound of them in a garden that no longer exists, a sound like a joyous dance, like bells ringing in the air. She told me that plants, animals, elements of nature, have a secret name, each and every one of them, that every flower hides this secret name in its petals, a name assigned by creation. Knowing the name, hearing the vibration, is what reveals the true world to you. Can you hear it? I asked her. Sometimes, she said. What's the true world like? I wanted to know. Like this one, she said, only better. It's fascinating. Magical.

For days, maybe weeks, I've just been waiting for Lucía. For days, weeks, hours, I've just been waiting for the sound of her yellow voice, her wolf words. For days, I've just wanted to touch her skin, just wanted to smell her scent of a bird in flight.

We're immune to the rumors that keep saying Lucía is a witch who turns into a cockroach at night. Because the lies evolve, change form, grow. The deceit envelops us like an invisible serpent devouring itself. But where does the serpent, inside the serpent's stomach, inside itself, go?

The unworthy and the servants give Lucía looks of fear and resentment, admiration and panic.

During the day we don't draw attention to ourselves, we hide what we do so the unworthy and the servants don't see it, so they don't know that at night we become the sound of flowers no longer in existence, that without words, using only our touch, we seek the secret names that vibrate in each other's skin. We pretend, so the Superior Sister suspects nothing, that each of us does not know the other's body, centimeter by centimeter. We feign normalcy so the unworthy don't learn of the words we whisper to each other, our lips so close, without kissing, without touching, until we can take it no longer. The words wrap around us, caress us, they're like the gentlest of rivers flowing over our bodies. The few times we've sat together in the Chapel of Ascension, our fingers have touched, but only under our tunics. At mealtime we sit apart, ignoring each other while thinking that when everyone else is asleep, we'll be naked and together, together in our tree.

I know the only one who suspects anything is Lourdes. She looks at us silently, slowly moving those hands of hers, black, venomous insects.

*   *   *

Metallic woods.

In our tree, I told Lucía what happened in the metallic woods.

We cried with our arms around each other. She comforted me, stroked my hair very slowly. We cried for Circe, for the girl I was, and for my pain, which hasn't faded, which still clings to me, remains deep inside me, and for all the years I could recall none of this, none of what they'd done to me, none of what I'd lived through before coming to the House of the Sacred Sisterhood.

*   *   *

I told Lucía that we'd left the town, gotten away from that animal, that thing, from the sad woman. For days, we'd walked in search of food, shelter, water. Lucía also remembers having walked alone, thirsty, with a ferocious thirst, she told me. She remembers having walked until she fainted. When I ask her about her life before the House of the Sacred Sisterhood, she says little or nothing, as though it hurts to remember.

I told her that we'd eventually found a strange building. It was in the middle of nowhere, surrounded by nothing. It had solar panels on the roof. When we entered it, I thought it might have once been a school or college. I tried to turn on the lights but they didn't work. Most of the solar panels had been broken by tornados, hail, floods, fire. There were chairs piled up, broken, one on top of the other, impossibly balanced, precarious. A whole wall covered in useless chairs. Circe took off running and minutes later returned with a rat between her teeth. Her capacity to hunt amazed me, she was quick, lethal, but she hadn't hunted anything in days. It was a medium-sized rat without much meat.

I tried to remove one of the chairs very carefully. I didn't want the mountain to collapse, but it did. I picked through the broken pieces for wood to make fire and cook the prey, the portion Circe had given me. We'd never broken that pact, no matter how hungry we were. We shared everything. But before eating, I wanted to explore while there was still light coming in through the broken windows. I needed to know if it was safe to spend the night. All I found were empty rooms or classrooms, most with chalkboards covered in formulas that no one had been able to erase. A few were stained with something red, something that had been thrown at the wall.

At the end of a hallway there was a locked door. It took me several attempts to pick the lock with my knife. In the room, I found books covered in mold and gnawed at by rats. Books of incomprehensible formulas. Nor did I understand most of the words that explained or talked about the formulas. I found a box of mobile phones that were turned off. My mother had told me about them, from when there was internet, she'd said. When the world still believed the internet was going to last forever. Now the phones are worthless. Black screens and silence. That's what Mom had said, black screens and silence, and she'd showed me her useless mobile, told me what the world had been like before, how people had done everything on those screens, how they believed that in some countries the electricity had been cut because of artificial intelligence, to prevent its advance, the spread of its power, its independence and hunger to dominate its creator. How after the final blackout the world did not recover, rebuild, restart, because nature finished things off with a new degree of devastation.

I didn't remember this because I was a newborn, a tiny human who had arrived in a world in pieces, a world where entire continents, islands, countries were now below water.

I don't really understand what artificial intelligence is about. It was something intangible, Mom told me, that controlled a large part of the world. She said there were groups of people who worshipped it.

In the room, a dusty bed was still made up with sheets, and there were a few cans of food on what looked like a desk. I stifled a cry of joy when I saw them. Those cans meant we would not die of hunger. Some of the labels were torn, but I guessed that one of the cans contained pickles, because I could make out part of the word: pick. The photo was so faded that the pickles were no longer green. The second can had a fish drawn on it that was maybe tuna or something else I couldn't have guessed or known. The last two had intact Campbell's Soup labels on them: one was tomato, the other cream of chicken. Since the expiration dates were illegible, I looked the cans over carefully and saw that none were rusted or swollen. This was a good indication to open them and smell what was inside, like the tarantula kids used to do. I'd never tried any of those foods before, and I never would.

In a locked cabinet, which I also picked, I found water bottles that were empty, except for one. Next to the bed, on a night table with a broken lamp, there was a black notebook that had writing in it. On the first pages, the handwriting was restrained, it respected the lines, the words were measured, like "concern," "how much can it rain in a day?" "wildfires and drought," "abrupt changes in temperature," "whales are dying, 30 found on the coast in the south." But then the notebook was pure rage, odd words like "CHAOS," "CATASTROPHE," "GLOBAL BLACKOUT," "END OF HUMANITY," "WHAT DID WE DO WITH OUR WORLD?" written in capital letters, in red ink, gone over again and again, as though tracing them until the paper had worn thin would change things, make the world inhabitable again. After that there were prayers to someone called the Lady of Thought, Goddess of Ideas, Queen of Reason, Absolute Artificial Intelligence. On another page, there was a drawing of a woman with an owl on her shoulder and the initials A.I. Was artificial intelligence a woman with an owl? The person who had written in the notebook begged to understand, begged for knowledge to face what was to come. There was no prayer to the erroneous God, which at the time was the only God I had known. After that there was nothing. Blank pages.

That night we drank a bit of water from the bottle. I'd boiled it first in a bowl because I couldn't trust even bottled water. I also ate the pieces of rat that Circe had given me. When I decided to open one of the cans to smell the food, to see if we could eat it, we heard noises.

*   *   *

I don't want to write what happens next, but I will, because the words these pages contain are like drops, small drops of black, ochre, blue, red, that dilute, briefly, the torment, the pain like silent fury.

*   *   *

We heard noises. I put out the fire and covered it like the tarantula kids had taught me, without leaving a trace, then I stuck the cans, bowls, and bottle in my makeshift satchel, picked up Circe, who squirmed as she always did when I grabbed her suddenly, and we hid in the room, under the bed. There were men, talking loudly, shouting. I heard their steps, the sound of them going through the bottles in the cabinet, throwing them to the floor in a rage because they were empty. The men were not methodical, they didn't even look under the bed. I was silently thankful for their ineptitude.

They grabbed the mobiles and pretended to call each other, laughing wildly, and it was as though their laughter contained only violence. Then they threw the mobiles to the floor, stepped on them, broke them.

From the different tones of voice, I figured there were three, maybe four men. They smelled very bad. We all smelled bad after days of walking under the sun, after months without washing. But these men smelled like corpses, like dried blood and rotten flesh. They stank like the adults who killed my friends, the tarantula kids, a filthy smell of rancid flesh hanging from murderous teeth.

Circe curled up in fear. I put her under my shirt and protected her with my body. After the men were gone, we fell asleep together.

The next day we left in case they returned. I put the cans away, thinking I'd ration the food, make another fire where we were safe, eat something there, just a bite, from one of the cans.

After walking for several hours, we found ourselves in the metallic woods. There were many trees, but the woods was small. It saddened me, and later I understood this was because they'd tried, in a sense, to imitate the beauty of real trees, and all that had resulted was crude structures, painted in colors that had faded over time. There had been no electricity for years, not since the great and final black-out. The trees were useless; they occupied a useless space. That was where it happened. In that useless place. In that useless space. Nothing grew there, it was just infertile earth and false trees.

I thought Circe had heard a noise and gone off to explore, but I didn't want to stay there. I sensed something insane in that woods, something dormant, lurking. I felt cold, though it was hot. I called Circe to leave and that was when they grabbed me. They must have been hiding behind the trees, because I hadn't heard or seen them. There were four men. I stabbed one in the leg with my knife. That infuriated them, and they threw me to the ground and struck me. I didn't feel the punches, all I wanted was for Circe to stay away, exploring, for her never to appear.

I pressed my hands into the infertile earth, grabbed a fistful, and threw it at them. One of the men laughed, the other wiped the earth from his eyes and took off my belt. I thought he was going to hit me harder, but then he ripped my shirt and lowered my pants. I'd never been naked in front of the tarantula kids. We respected each other's privacy, looked after one another. I tried to cover myself with my hands, to hide my naked body with the strips of cloth that always hung from my neck, and I spat at them, but while one of them hit me, the other tied my hands with the cloth. Then he took the belt and struck me, furious, taking pleasure in it. He smiled as he hit me.

Circe appeared, silently, lethal, and leapt onto one of the men's backs, biting and scratching him. But there were too many of them. My enchantress, my little sorceress, couldn't fight them all. I screamed and tried to help Circe. I was able to free one of my hands and I scratched, kicked, tried to bite them, but they hit me so many times

I fainted. The last thing I saw was Circe's eyes, I saw the rabid ocean, the sea of savage stars fighting desperately, but behind the constellations, there was no rage, only an eternal dance of light.

I don't know how I survived; I don't know how I was able to pick myself up. They thought I was dead, otherwise they would have used me until they'd killed me, like the adults did with the kids that were part of their group, the adults that murdered my tarantula brothers and sisters, because they couldn't trap us. The men had left. They hadn't even bothered to tie my hands again because they thought I wouldn't wake up. They stole my satchel with the water, bowls, cans, and my knife. I didn't care about any of that. I just wanted to find Circe. I got up as best I could, blood between my legs, barely able to walk. I fell and couldn't move, I was in so much pain. On the ground, I straightened my clothes, tied my destroyed shirt with some strips of cloth I'd found, and tried to cover my naked body. I dragged myself along the infertile earth. I shouted her name.

Circe

C   i   r   c   e

Circe

until I saw her. She was lying in the middle of the useless woods, with its useless trees. She looked smaller and so fragile. I dragged myself painfully until I reached her body and touched it. She was dead. They had stabbed her too many times to count.

I didn't cry.

Circe's eyes were open and the sky was still there, held by her gaze. I rested my face on the body of my enchantress, against her soft fur, and remained there, without moving, waiting for her magical sound, the vibration that made me smile. I hugged her for hours as her body grew cold. I sang her a song without words.

When I was able to get up, I took Circe in my arms and wandered aimlessly, my clothes tattered, stained with blood, hers and mine, two bodies broken, hers and mine.

I came to a dry river. On its banks stood a tree that looked dead, though I noticed a shoot growing, barely visible. A tiny stem with a small, green leaf. I decided that's where my Circe would rest. I put her down very carefully, and with my aching, useless hands, the hands that had been unable to save her, I began to dig. The earth was hard, like stone, but I didn't stop until my fingers bled. The hole was deep enough so that no animal would unbury her. I knew the chances were slim because there were fewer and fewer animals, but I would allow no one to touch her. No one could touch her. I placed her in the ground very slowly, closed her eyes, that immense sky, and covered her with dry earth.

I rested my head against her grave. I was crying so hard I think I fainted. After that, I don't know what happened, what I did, how many days, weeks, years, I walked alone over the ravaged earth, I don't know how I arrived, half-dead, dragging myself, to the House of the Sacred Sisterhood.

*   *   *

These words also exist because of Circe, so I don't forget her, so I can hear the magical sound my enchantress made, the subtle vibration that slips between the folds and curves of these clandestine letters. If I close my eyes, I hear it, because she's with me, though her body is in the earth, in that tree I imagine to be green and in bloom.

*   *   *

In our hollow, where we were isolated, protected, Lucía told me she'd dreamed of a place with a lake, trees, green mountains. A place outside the House of the Sacred Sisterhood.

It's just a dream, I told her. Outside there's endless desert, a ravaged world.

The dream was real. I also dreamed of you before coming here, that's why I knew I had to come, that's why I was so startled when I first saw you in the woods, because you were the woman in my dream.

I inhaled and the night air filled my lungs. Was the world outside the House of the Sacred Sisterhood recovering? Could survival be possible without the Enlightened?

*   *   *

The tongueless mouth. That was the first thing I saw through my veil, the black, open mouth. A hole emptied of words. The Diaphanous Spirit was lying near the crops, her arms in a cross, her white tunic stained with blood. Her hands were rigid, and we saw marks on her wrists, as though she'd been tied up for a long time. Her fingers were bruised, her nails broken. On her neck there were lesions, gashes, wounds. Her body was motionless, and we could now see her slightly swollen belly. With her motionless eyes, she looked up at the motionless sky that had flecks of orange in it. I moved my veil to see better and noticed the tiny, glittering body of a fire ant crawl out of her tongueless mouth. The ant walked over the Diaphanous Spirit's open eyes, lingered on her black pupil, and got lost in her lashes.

We were on our way back from the woods and the sun was already rising. We're very cautious when we return at dawn, because Diaphanous Spirits tend to wander through the garden, or among the crops, to listen to the first sounds of the day, the hidden signs in the air, in the earth. That's why we wear our veils, in case anyone sees us, so we can flee without being recognized.

Her expression suggested she was absorbed in deep, important thought. In some divine, decoded message. But beneath that expression was another, maybe awe contained within fear, maybe desperation. By the light that enters through the crack in my cell, the light that allows me to write these words, I wonder why Diaphanous Spirits look for messages in the earth if He despises the earth, considers it impure, contaminated with sin. Why does the Superior Sister allow it? Without faith, there is no refuge.

We saw the tongueless mouth and we saw a white butterfly perch on one of the Diaphanous Spirit's hands. I thought it strange that the butterfly's legs didn't burn her dead skin, that it was free of contamination. It moved its wings, quivering slightly, and for a moment the white turned gray. Then we watched in silence as the butterfly flew away.

Lucía tried to touch the Diaphanous Spirit, but I told her not to, said we should return to our cells so we wouldn't be seen; the others would be waking by now, I said, and we should let them find her, so they didn't accuse us of having killed her. Lucía moved her veil, lifted the Diaphanous Spirit's tunic slightly, and we saw her legs stained with blood. Red threads, still wet. Lucía looked at me, and something in her eyes made me think she understood, that she knew what I suspected, that the Diaphanous Spirit was full of sin and had tried to escape punishment but had not survived.

We heard a scream—or a howl? a bird cry? a wail?—and we split up to return to our cells without being seen. But when I saw that Lucía was gone, I went back to the Diaphanous Spirit and took off her sacred crystal.

The light that comes in through the crack tells me the sun is out. I see the tongueless mouth as I write, the mouth capable, with its emptiness, of destroying the world.

*   *   *

Strange days. Days of confinement.

Absolute silence. We've been told not to speak. Ever since the announcement, in the Chapel of Ascension, that a Diaphanous Spirit had left for the intangible dimension. We're to mourn her disappearance with complete silence, and to fast.

The hunger doesn't bother us, we're all used to eating little or nothing, we were all wanderers, but we've been confined to our cells until further notice. The crevice in the wall tells me night is approaching, that it's cool outside. That there's no moon.

I struggle to write, now that I can, now that I have this time by myself, with these pages and without interruption or threat. I struggle because I need to see Lucía, to hear her voice shining in the dark of the woods.

Hours pass and I write only a few lines.

Through the crevice, I feel the temperature change as the days pass. It's cold now, a cold that forces me to write under the blanket. I don't think I'll be able to sleep in my bed tonight, or anytime soon, because I got used to being with Lucía, my arms wrapped around her, even if it was for only a few nocturnal hours. I know she's thinking about me, as I am about her.

I wonder what they'll have done with the Diaphanous Spirit's body. I wonder how they'll have carried the corpse, who helped the Superior Sister. Lourdes, maybe? Will they have buried her or hidden her?

I wonder if they'll have closed her tongueless mouth.

I wonder if they'll have closed her eyes, those eyes looking up at the sky. If the fire ant is still trapped in her lashes, if it was detained in a gaze that can no longer see.

What could have happened to the other Chosen? Why tell us they get trapped in a different dimension? Could they have killed them? Were they the ones who killed the Minor Saint? They were.

* * *

Three days passed before they opened the cells. Some of the unworthy drank water from the basins we use to wash, water from the Creek of Madness. But I endured the hunger and thirst.

At breakfast no one spoke. We were nervous; we gave each other looks of veiled suspicion and accusation, the result of having been confined. We were wary too. They'd never locked us in our cells. Why now? the others wondered silently. But Lucía and I knew, we knew it was so they could deal with the Diaphanous Spirit's body.

It took a lot of effort not to look at Lucía. Instead I looked at Lourdes, who was radiant, strangely radiant. Later I would learn why. I would come to understand all the harm she wanted to cause. She had fed the rumor. She had filled it with thorns, venom, fury. The rumor grew and took shape, a dangerous shape. I don't know how she did it when we were all confined to our cells. The unworthy and the servants had begun to whisper that Lucía had used her witch's powers, her dark, ancestral magic, against one of our Chosen, and she had succeeded, we had lost her because Lucía had hexed her, betrayed her by contacting ominous forces. Now she was trapped in the intangible dimension and the refuge provided us by the House of the Sacred Sisterhood was at risk. Communication with our God was under threat.

I would also come to understand why no one sat next to Lucía at breakfast. She ate the lumpy, white mixture with her back upright, unperturbed.

But I was perturbed. So I went to the woods to look for amanitas.

*   *   *

Last night we saw Lourdes dance naked in the garden. The cold moonlight cast fiery flecks in her red hair. It was a red that wounded, the frozen heart of the sun.

We were not supposed to be in the garden at night, but no one told the Superior Sister because we were mesmerized by Lourdes's white body, the ecstatic look on her face, her arms raised to the sky, her lips slightly parted, her legs moving to the rhythm of music only she could hear. She was beautiful when she enjoyed herself, when she wasn't plotting. When she danced naked and free, her hands moved like a bird's feathers in the wind, fluttering gently, not like deadly insects.

She'd eaten the cricket bread mixed with amanita, a gift I'd left on the pillow in her cell. Her weaklings, her disciples, leave her offerings now and then. That's why she didn't suspect a thing.

We saw her laugh, we saw her intimate, personal celebration. Her sacred dance.

For a moment, I thought she was happy.

Then she began to scream at nothing, at everyone: The moon, the moon, the moon is telling me secrets, she knows about the monks, the dead monks that haunt us, that curse us. The moon, the moon has power.

Turning in circles, Lourdes went up to Lucía, stopped in front of her, and in a voice intended to threaten, but that was weak, almost sad, she said: Witch, witch of the night, witch of the moon.

Unexpectedly, she hugged Lucía, and repeated, like a mantra:

Witch, witch of the night, witch of the moon

Witch, witch of the night, witch of the moon, beautiful witch, my witch

Lucía walked Lourdes to her cell, dressed her in her nightgown, laid her down, and tucked her in.

I admired Lucía's capacity for mercy, but it also angered me. It filled me with rage that she forgave Lourdes, who only wanted to do her harm.

One of the servants said she was going to call the Superior Sister, but we threatened to punish her in the Tower of Silence for something she hadn't done, for harming some animal we'd never seen, or stealing eggs we'd never eaten. The Superior Sister wouldn't question our word and the servant knew it.

Later that night, Lucía and I went to the woods and she didn't reproach me at all. She didn't ask why I'd drugged Lourdes or make me feel guilty. I'd told her about the amanita's effects. I think she understood I was trying to protect her.

We were in each other's arms in the hollow when we heard noises and were startled. The unworthy and the servants don't dare enter the thicket, the density of the woods, at night. This was where the blasphemous, the brash, were buried. Steps, orders, whispers. From the dark hollow we saw two figures, one of them stumbling. An unworthy. Her white nightgown was visible in the dark; the servants don't wear nightgowns. The other figure was colossal, so colossal it could only have been the Superior Sister.

The sky was cloudy, but for an instant we could make out Lourdes's red hair in the moonlight. She was still under the effects of the amanita; she kept falling, and the Superior Sister picked her up and shook her. We saw her throw Lourdes against a tree and raise her nightgown. Then she pressed her crazed body against Lourdes's white, solitary body, which was writhing. We saw her break off a branch and force Lourdes to her hands and knees, like a dog. We saw her remove Lourdes's nightgown and slowly run the branch over her back, as though she was caressing her, before she struck her and caressed her, caressed her and struck her. Lourdes laughed. This seemed to enrage the Superior Sister, who struck her harder.

Lourdes laughed louder, cackling, almost howling. She howled like a she-wolf, or like I imagine a she-wolf would howl. Then the Superior Sister put the branch around her neck and began to tighten it. She wanted to shut Lourdes up, but she also wanted to kill her. Lucía looked at me, and though she didn't say a word, I knew what she was going to do, and that I wouldn't let her do it alone. We covered ourselves with our veils and left the hollow stealthily. Each of us grabbed a branch from the ground, one of the many branches in the woods, feeling around in the dark for whatever was available, though the moonlight shone when we needed it as though it knew its daughters were in danger.

I ran up to the Superior Sister from behind and struck her on the head with the branch. Lucía struck her in the kidneys. The Superior Sister doubled over in pain, though she didn't fall, and then we hit her again and again and again, and when she was on the ground, having fainted or possibly died, we grabbed Lourdes, and as we put her nightgown back on, the three of us ran through the woods toward our cells.

But the Superior Sister doesn't die. That's what everyone says. They say she's so resilient she could be immortal. Which is why when we woke, Lourdes was hanging from a tree in the woods, visible from the garden. Around her neck was a rope tied to a high branch. Her body swayed back and forth as though in a useless dance. It was the wind. A storm was coming. Her red hair covered her face, then blew off to the side to reveal her open eyes. Her white nightgown was stained with earth and her feet were bare and dirty.

I couldn't scream out loud, but on the inside I was crying, wailing, the pain coursing through my bones. I was surprised to feel all this. I didn't care about Lourdes, but she didn't deserve that death.

The Superior Sister unleashed all her rage on one of her favorites among the unworthy, on a candidate for Enlightened, because Lourdes was too perfect to be Chosen. How much anger, how much rage she must have felt to have killed her like that. We know this wrath is just the beginning, that someone else is going to pay.

There was no breakfast. The servants took clear pleasure in informing us that we were all to go to the Chapel of Ascension when the bells tolled.

I write while I wait. I write in the monks' blue ink, the monks He and the Superior Sister murdered. Through the crevice I can already smell the humidity in the air, the rain approaching.

These could be my last words. We know the veils protect our identity, but the Superior Sister has spies, her power lies in dividing us. And she's going to seek revenge.

*　　　*　　　*

He was behind the chancel screen, but He didn't speak to us. We felt His presence. María de las Soledades covered her mouth so she wouldn't cough. She'd been frail for weeks, barely eating, and had long stopped speaking. The Superior Sister was at the altar. Though we couldn't see her, we heard her boots strike the floor. It was anger, it was rage, it was violence that we perceived in those strikes. We couldn't see Him either, but we heard a grunt, and the Superior Sister went still. Then the silence was total. We didn't even hear the storm, the water battering the stained glass, hounding the white deer in its luscious garden. We didn't even think about Lourdes's body being bashed against the trees. Swaying back and forth, her wet nightgown stuck to her skin. Her bare feet washed by the water that fell from the sky. Nor did we hear the rain drop into the buckets the servants had put out. The silence solidified the air. None of us dared make the slightest movement, but I was next to Lucía, and under our tunics I brought my hand to hers. I didn't care about the silence or about what could happen to me. I didn't care about the Superior Sister or about Him or the Enlightened; I just wanted to return to the woods, for Lucía and me to discover the secret music of every plant, every tree.

María de las Soledades couldn't stop herself from coughing. The Superior Sister got down from the altar. She was holding the whip with the leather thongs. There was no need for her to hit María de las Soledades, who got to her feet, positioned herself in front of the Superior Sister, and lowered her head, waiting for punishment. This seemed to make the Superior Sister angrier, and she shook María de las Soledades and yelled: "Go to the Tower of Silence with no food or water. Go to the Tower of Silence now, under surveillance, until I say so." She raised her whip, but since María de las Soledades just looked at her, resigned, or tired, or indifferent, the Superior Sister struck the floor and ordered two servants to take her there, lock the door, and keep watch until further notice.

We'd never seen her out of control, she'd never shown us that a situation had gotten the best of her. But María de las Soledades's indifference overwhelmed her. She screamed at us to stand in a row. Chaotically, without really understanding, we formed two rows facing each other between the pews. She walked along the rows, looking at us one by one, striking her whip on the tiled floor. We kept our eyes straight ahead and tried to appear impassive, except for Catalina, who lowered her gaze. The Superior Sister pulled her out of the line. Catalina trembled. Lucía looked at me and almost stepped forward, but I grabbed her hand, stopped her. She wanted to save Catalina, but Catalina was already in the Superior Sister's clutches. She kept walking and stopped in front of Élida, who was crying. She looked at her for a long time. Élida had been one of María de las Soledades's weaklings, she was too fragile for this world. She struggled to learn the House of the Sacred Sisterhood's language, which is why we almost never heard her speak. The Superior Sister bent down and inspected her tunic, saw that it was stained with earth. She ordered two servants to remove Catalina and Élida from the Chapel of Ascension. We knew she was going to take her time with them. But she would do so later.

She ordered us to sit down. When she stepped onto the altar, she returned to her chair and raised an arm, pointing to one of the stained glass windows that faced the garden, the one with the white deer.

He began to speak. He said that what the Enlightened had seen was horrifically clear. They had seen that one of the unworthy, the one hanging from the tree for being defiant, for being an infected channel of insolence, an outbreak of depravity that spread all the earth's misfortune, that this unworthy had conspired to trap a Diaphanous Spirit in the intangible dimension.

It was as though His voice were beneath a frozen sea, trying to break the eternal ice. But it could not, because His vibrating words were wordless, emptied of meaning, dismembered and dispersed particles of sound. He continued to speak, for hours or minutes that went on too long. While He ranted, I stroked Lucía's skin under our tunics to calm her, so she wouldn't try to save us all, each and every one of us, sacrificing herself. But I stopped when I heard Him say in a different voice: "The Chosen have announced the advent of a new Enlightened one."

The unworthy suppressed a cry of joy, but when a murmur rose, the Superior Sister permitted it. The murmur spread throughout the Chapel of Ascension. Some of the unworthy hugged, but I was petrified, paralyzed. I couldn't stop myself from looking at Lucía. She was looking at me too, and in her eyes I saw fear.

* * *

We heard screams in the night. Catalina and Élida.

Some of the servants say the Superior Sister locked them in dog cages. Cages so small they can't move. They say she wants them to live on all fours, crawling, trained to eat out of bowls, bark, attack insubordinates. The servants whisper that Catalina and Élida have begged to be killed, for someone to put an end to their martyrdom. I've never seen those cages. I've never seen any dogs. Others say Catalina and Élida are dead.

* * *

It's been three days and we still don't know who the new Enlightened one is. We're anxious.

Some of the unworthy have increased their hours of sacrifice. We hear self-flagellation, blood atonement, floggings against flesh, in the hope it will improve their chances of becoming Enlightened.

Lucía and I had planned to meet in the woods, but we couldn't without taking Lourdes's body down from the tree. We couldn't leave her there. It had stopped raining, though drops still fell from her white nightgown. We wouldn't leave her there. Even though that's what the Superior Sister wants, for Lourdes to hang from the tree for days as a reminder, threat, and punishment.

I took off my veil and climbed the tree, despite the danger. When I reached the branch, I untied the rope. I knew we could be burned alive, but I did it anyways. Lourdes's body fell into the wet grass almost without a sound, as though it had been emptied out.

Lucía knelt on the ground and put her left arm under Lourdes's neck and her right under her knees. She cradled her. They were so pale they looked like a living sculpture. There was no pain on Lourdes's face. Her eyes were open and Lucía gazed at her as though she were alive.

I put on my veil and we entered the woods. We carried the body together, carefully, solemnly, sadly. The sky was full of stars. I remembered my mother saying that the great blackout caused a global collapse, worse than an earthquake or the eruption of a volcano. But the only positive thing, Mom had said, was that in the cities they saw the stars again.

With branches, our hands, stones, we spent hours digging a grave. Lucía said nothing about my responsibility or blame. That's why I kissed her when we were done. She understood I was thankful for her silence. Before we placed Lourdes in the grave, I took out the sacred crystal I'd stolen from the Diaphanous Spirit and put it around her neck, very carefully, as though she could feel it. I let her open eyes take in the stars. We said nothing, no prayer; we were silent as we contemplated the sky with Lourdes. Then I closed her eyes and we covered her with earth.

In the dark, we went to the Creek of Madness to clean the dirt from our faces, from under our nails, in our hair. It was cold, but Lucía took off her tunic and washed it, and I did the same. There we were. Naked in the water of madness. Hugging in the insanity. Kissing each other in the folly. Stroking each other in the irrationality. Together in the wild water.

We whispered our real names in the cool creek, under the moon.

When we saw the stars disappearing, we put on our veils and wet tunics and ran to our cells. That's when Lucía said she wanted to save María de las Soledades. I told her it was dangerous, but she said we'd wait until the servants were no longer keeping watch, that we could enter the Tower of

Silence then. She also said she didn't want to be Enlightened because she wouldn't see me anymore, because she
didn't want Him to touch her. I hugged her as though it
could protect her.

We didn't have breakfast, instead offering to make a
sacrifice. We'd tend to the crops and accompany a Diaphanous Spirit. The others smiled at Lucía and ignored me.
Our tunics were still damp, and we wanted them to dry in
the sun. The heat was extreme.

We noticed the plants were stronger, their green almost
gleaming, but we said nothing, just exchanged surprised
looks.

We learned that at breakfast the Superior Sister had
been inspecting the unworthy's hands, looking under their
nails. She wanted to find out who had buried Lourdes, who
had defied her by lowering Lourdes's body from the tree.

By the time the Superior Sister reached the crops with
Lourdes's weaklings, our tunics were dry and our hands
clean because we hadn't turned the soil, just pruned the
sick leaves. We lowered our heads, as is expected in the
Superior Sister's presence, and she gave us a long look.
One of Lourdes's weaklings said something in her ear, and
she focused her eyes on Lucía. They wanted revenge. Lucía
would have to pay for it all. The Superior Sister said nothing, just gave Lucía a new look, one I hadn't seen before.

There was a dark light in her eyes, a dangerous epiphany, a powerful revelation.

The Superior Sister opened her mouth to say something but closed it when we all heard a buzzing sound. It was a bee. The first we'd seen in a long time. There were wasps in the woods, but the bee made me question, again, whether the world outside the House of the Sacred Sisterhood was beginning to recover.

They still haven't announced who will be Enlightened.

*　　　*　　　*

The rumors about Lucía subsided until they disappeared. The unworthy have been very busy with flagellations and sacrifices to increase their chances of being the next Enlightened. Some have decided to clean the floor with their tongues. We see them crouched down, their tongues black, and they're sick, ill from all the filth they've swallowed, but they go on cleaning because their sacrifice must be absolute.

Others have been fasting on their knees in the hallways or in the garden and have fainted from hunger.

*　　　*　　　*

We had to wait three days before rescuing María de las Soledades. The Superior Sister blamed one of Lourdes's weaklings for burying her body. She was made to take off her tunic and lie on broken glass in her white nightgown. A minor punishment. Has the Superior Sister's anger dissipated? Or is she exhausted from torturing Catalina and Élida? She threw a blue cup, a cup of frosted glass. It was beautiful, singular, had no doubt belonged to the monks. She destroyed it. Then she broke others that were just as beautiful. Lourdes's weakling lay on the blue glass for hours, but she didn't cry, she offered to take the punishment as a sacrifice. Her longing to be Enlightened was clear in everything she did.

As I write these words in ochre ink, I wait to see Lucía, because tonight we're going to rescue María de las Soledades. The Superior Sister wants her to die in the Tower of Silence. I'm thinking we'll hide her until she regains her strength. After that I don't know what we'll do. The first step is to rescue her.

Lucía has made me feel things I've forgotten, like mercy. It's no longer silent dynamite, but something else; it's like a new heart, beating inside the old one.

*　　*　　*

Last night I picked the lock on the door to the Tower of Silence. Lucía kept watch, holding a glass bottle full of water. I was surprised by the silence. The crickets weren't chirping, there was no excruciating music, no maddening song capable of cornering you into insanity. We saw a black figure in the night sky. It took us a while to realize the enormous wings were those of a vulture. We rejoiced, because vultures had disappeared years, decades ago. At that moment, I thought about telling Lucía that we should escape too, that we might find life outside the House of the Sacred Sisterhood, but I didn't say anything because I had to hurry and pick the lock. We realized the vulture was flying in circles, as vultures tend to do, waiting for María de las Soledades to die.

We climbed the eighty-eight steps and opened the hatch. The stench of decay struck us. It was so strong I felt it in my mouth, tasted on my tongue the blood that runs through death's veins. We stepped on the bones of Chosen who had died long ago. I wondered how many Diaphanous Spirits, how many Full Auras and Minor Saints had disintegrated in the Tower of Silence. The bones broke with a hollow sound. It was hot. The smell of rot was coming from the Minor Saint's body. Her bones didn't yet glow like the rest of them, they didn't give off the white light we sometimes see rising from the Tower of Silence.

María de las Soledades was there among the bones.
We said her name, whispered it, but she didn't answer.
Lucía told me her pulse was too weak, that it was barely
detectable. I lifted María de las Soledades to give her water,
so she wouldn't choke, and then Lucía tried wetting her fingers and running them over her lips. But she didn't react.
Very carefully, Lucía brought the bottle to her mouth to
give her a sip of water.

The vulture continued to fly in circles, coming closer
and closer.

Lucía laid María de las Soledades back down, and it
was then that she opened her eyes. We took off our veils,
but I can't be certain she recognized us, nor that she really
saw us. She looked at the sky, the vulture, and smiled with
her perforated, wounded, silenced mouth. I regretted not
having helped her earlier, not having talked to her, having
belittled her, which is why, when she stopped breathing,
I touched the scars on her mouth, closed her eyes, and
cried. Lucía took my hands so I wouldn't feel so alone in
my personal atonement.

We heard a sound, like a chant, only heinous. We
looked at the sky and saw the vulture still flying, relentless.
I felt a chill. Lucía gave me a frightened look. The vulture
won't attack us, I said, but she whispered in my ear that it
wasn't a vulture, that the monks were here, watching us,

that they wanted to see us fall from up high, to kill us with their voices in the dark. I hugged her, unsure what to say.

We left the Tower of Silence feeling faint, dejected.

*　　　*　　　*

Lucía is the new Enlightened one.

I'm not crying, but tears are falling inside me, wounding me. I want to scream, red sand is gathering in my blood, accumulating in my throat, sand like a tornado of lava, a cyclone of scalding water.

But I can't scream. It's as though I had earth in my mouth, like Helena.

*　　　*　　　*

The ceremony was held during the day. Lucía had been under guard since the Enlightened had made the announcement.

We couldn't go to the woods, I couldn't say goodbye, say her real name, very slowly, so close to her lips we were almost touching. I couldn't hug her. Or smell her again, her scent like a cloudless sky.

I write these useless words, these words that can't open the carved black door, the Refuge of the Enlightened, which is where she is now, because they've already taken her there.

The servants told us to wash and handed each of us a clean white tunic. We all knew what that meant. There was anticipation in the air, and maybe joy; expectation and something like a silent celebration. The unworthy smiled as they brushed each other's hair, except for Lucía and I. We gave each other furtive looks of suppressed anguish.

We went to the Chapel of Ascension, the sun entering through the stained glass, adorning the walls and floor with different-colored lights, though the tones were subdued, muted.

There were real flowers. I wondered where they were from. The few flowers that grew in the garden were pale in color, sickly. The vase was small, but the bouquet seemed huge; branches of green leaves had been added to it, and the red, yellow, and orange flowers stood out so much they seemed unreal. Had they been picked outside the House of the Sacred Sisterhood?

I sat down by Lucía's side and took her hand. Our tunics covered us. We were nervous.

He was behind the chancel screen. All we saw of the Superior Sister was her boots striking the wood floor.

Two Minor Saints were led inside by servants. Their eyes were sewn shut correctly; there was no risk of bleeding or fainting. This job, sewing the Minor Saints' eyes, had no doubt been the offering, the sacrifice, of one of the unworthy, who had learned from Mariel not to make mistakes. The sacred crystals hanging from their necks gleamed in the sunlight, but the glare hurt my eyes and I had to lower my head. The Minor Saints sang the Hymn of the Enlightened, the most cherished hymn of all, but I wasn't paying attention. The unworthy looked at each other, hypnotized by the song.

A Full Aura appeared at the altar. She couldn't hear the Hymn of the Enlightened because she'd been mutilated, because she's deaf, because her eardrums have been perforated, but she danced, or tried to imitate dancing, and it looked as though she was trembling, as though her body was convulsing. On her hands and feet there were marks, wounds that hadn't healed or that someone had prevented from healing. They looked infected. I couldn't see her aura of fire, but I heard her voice, we all did. It was like a sea of silence, washing away all words, all thought.

She got down from the altar and pointed to Lucía.

I squeezed Lucía's hand under the tunic. I felt like I couldn't breathe. She looked at me, and without having to say the words, she asked for help. She asked with her eyes, her skin, the secret language of her body.

The unworthy gave her looks of admiration and hatred.

Then two Diaphanous Spirits appeared with their empty mouths, their dark mouths, smiled at her, and took her away.

*   *   *

At night, I don't go to the woods, I rest my head on the carved black door and listen. Eight days have passed since I last saw her. For eight days I've heard screams behind the door, brief, broken cries, and roars like those of a predator baring his fangs.

I'm going to get her out of there.

I'll keep these pages very near my heart, held in place by the fabric I'll wrap around my body, as I've done so many times.

Tonight I'm going to try to open the carved black door. I want to see how hard it is to pick the lock.

*   *   *

I write now in the monks' blue ink. I don't care if it runs out.

Yesterday, when everyone was asleep, and the silence was total, when I knew the hallways were empty, I walked barefoot to the Refuge of the Enlightened. I stopped when I heard the Superior Sister's steps. Steps that destroy the tiles, the earth, the life on which they tread. I had the knife I use to chip at the crack in the wall. It's like the one I carried when I picked locks with the tarantula kids. I opened the door to an empty cell near the carved black door, one that's never used. The lock was easy to pick, they must think no one would dare try. I heard the Superior Sister enter the Refuge of the Enlightened.

I stayed in the cell for a long time, hours. I needed to be sure she wasn't awake. When I got used to the dark, I thought I saw two boxes covered with sheets—or two cages? I thought I heard a moan, or a sob, like in a dream. But I decided not to check what or who was there. If it was Catalina and Élida, it was too late for them. My priority was Lucía.

When I was in front of the Refuge of the Enlightened, I was extremely careful to make as little noise as possible. It wasn't an easy lock—how could it have been? But Ulysses had taught me all the tricks, and after him I'd learned more too. It took me longer than expected, but once I understood the mechanism, I left without opening it. I don't want them to suspect anything. Now I know that when the time comes, it'll take me seconds.

Tomorrow is the day, tomorrow I'm going to get her out of there.

*   *   *

These words contain my pulse.

My breath.

The music that radiates from the blood flowing through my veins.

I'm in the tree hollow, in my woods. I understand now that the woods is not just trees, that it could never be reduced in that way; it's the subterranean, microscopic life, the aerial life, all that reverberates with the splendor of a living cathedral. The light that filters through the leaves forms translucent columns, a radiant sea expanding. I can feel the aura, the power that pulses through the air. I can touch it. I can caress the warm, gleaming particles of light with my fingertips. I'm part of this pagan temple, this ancestral sanctuary.

I write with the sharp point of a quill. A quill made with the feather of a bird that might be flying somewhere. It's blue, like the brilliant blue of swallows. These words are the color of my blood, mixed with dirt. Blood from the wound in my stomach.

When the first bell tolls, they'll come for us. They'll have trouble finding me because I'm in the thicket. It could take hours. There's no time to dig my grave, to let the roots grow through my skin, to wait for fruit or herbs or mushrooms to sprout from my decomposing body. There's no time to die looking at the star-filled sky.

I'm going to go on writing until the bells toll. Then I'll hide these pages, leave them behind. I'm going to take the stone I used to sharpen the quill, and I'm going to open my wound, so more blood flows. All of the blood in my veins will fall like a red dragon, and the earth will receive it, absorb and transform it.

I picked the lock and opened the black door of carved wood; I opened it slowly so I wouldn't be seen, and I saw what was forbidden; I saw the cogs of the lie, that there is no god, just his mouth insulting, just the hunger, just him and his hands, him and his voice of a sacred battalion, a blessed legion, a black wave that drags wails in its wake; and like in a static image that lasted a few seconds, I saw the enlightened swollen with sin, their wombs bursting with vice, and I wasn't surprised at the proof of what had been apparent, that he was profaning them; and I kept still as I looked for Lucía until I saw her underneath him, enduring the abominable ritual, the superior sister watching them, her back to me and her leather whip in one hand, and then I covered my mouth to stifle a scream, and Lucía moved her head and gave me a look of surprise, desperation, and helplessness, a gaze that gave me strength, and with sudden speed I stabbed the superior sister in the kidney with my knife, took away her whip and, with the handle, struck her in the nape of her neck, and in spite of her size, the blow was so hard she stumbled and fell, and then he stood up, naked, and tried to attack me, and for the first time I saw his face, a face with the horrific perfection of a sculpture, empty in a way that envelops you until it chokes you, and I hit him with the whip and hit him again and again, but some of the enlightened looked at me, uncomprehending, frightened, and they helped the superior sister up and she wounded me with my knife, through the fabric that held this book of the night, these pages, and Lucía pushed her and grabbed my hand, and as we escaped, I saw that some of the enlightened didn't understand what was happening, that others were trying to trap us, and a few had followed us.

We ran.

Despite the pain in my stomach, I was able to slide the quill into the lock on the black door and break it. They won't get out easily. It'll buy us time.

The fabric is stopping my blood from flowing. I think that's why I can write. Why I haven't fainted. Or is it the will to tell this story? So none of us, not Lucía, Circe, Helena, or myself, are lost to oblivion.

As we ran, others joined us, those who saw a way out, an opportunity. When we reached our tree I told Lucía to leave, to flee through the hole in the wall, the one she'd dug with her hands, to escape with the few enlightened, unworthy, and servants who had followed us. I'd stay behind to delay the progeny of filth, the mistakes of nature, the murderers that are the superior sister and that despicable man capable of lingering on my body. Lucía refused, begged me to escape with her, but I kissed her, stroked her black hair, hugged the blue paradise that she was, and told her I had no time left. I showed her the wound and she understood it was too deep. She hugged me back and wept until three of the enlightened tried to take her away. Lucía put up a fight. I told her they had to flee, that if they stayed, they'd be killed. Before they left, she hugged me again, and through her tears, she called me by my real name, kissed me one last time, and, in her translucent voice, said three words, but they weren't words, they were a vibration of fire, fire that enveloped me like a river of light, a river of dazzling flowers.

I'm going to leave this book of the night, these pages I've been writing and protecting for so long, in the hollow of the tree, our tree. Maybe one day someone will find them and read them, or they'll get wet and return to their origin, to the trees where they began, and these words will become the woods, will be purified by the sap, will glow in the roots. Or maybe they'll disintegrate into a void that caresses,

governs,

hurts.

I hear the bells. They're coming.

This book is dedicated to the Argentine writer Ángeles Salvador (1972–2022), who left us a body of work that's irreverent, lucid, and brilliant, like she was; and to all the indomitable, bewitching, disobedient women, to those who have the light.

Thank you to Liliana Díaz Mindurry, who has been my maestra, friend, and one of my favorite writers and humans since the age of nineteen, for her wise advice throughout the process of writing this and each of my books. Thank you to Félix Bruzzone, Sarah Moses, Willie Schavelzon, and Bárbara Graham for their attentive readings and generous support. Thank you especially to Magalí Etchebarne and Laura Mazzini, whose dedication, tireless work, and love of words helped me create a better version of this work.

Thank you to my family and friends for their ongoing support.

Thank you to Mariano, for being my love in this and every life.